The Adventures of Sage Hawkins

BY

SCARLETT HOFFMAN

All Rights Reserved

The Lost Fairy Chronicles Book I: The Adventures of Sage Hawkins © 2022 by Anatolian Press

This is a work of fiction. Names, characters, businesses, places, events, locales, and incidents are either the product of the author's imagination or used fictitiously. Any resemblance to actual persons, living or dead, or actual events is purely coincidental. No part of this book may be reproduced or used in any manner without the written permission of the copyright owner except for the use of quotations in a book review. For more information, email micah@anatolianpressllc.com

Cover Illustration by Audrey Hoffman-Davis

Interior Illustrations Sara Hageman

Book design and production by Anatolian Press, LLC

Editing by Anatolian Press

First paperback edition November 2022

eBook ISBN: 978-1-959396-03-1

Paperback ISBN: 978-1-959396-04-8

Please visit us at

www.anatolianpressllc.com

The Adventures Of
SAGE HAWKINS
The Lost Fairy Chronicles Book One

SCARLETT HOFFMAN

— *This book is dedicated to* —

My mom, who never stopped loving and supporting me.

My amazing teacher, Angelia Derrick, who helped me discover the wonders of writing.

My incredible cover designer, Audrey Hoffman-Davis and my wonderful illustrator, Sara Hageman. My book wouldn't be the same without you.

And to any kid who loves reading, never stop. Look at the world in a new perspective and live life like an adventure. Magic is real, you just have to look for it.

Chapters

Prologue..

The Interview 1

Days Blur Together 12

An Unexpected Meeting 15

A New Life 28

Official Member of the Fairies 32

The Cat Attacks 38

Party Girl 42

You're Late 47

Celebrity in a Day 49

My Friend Has Freaky Powers 54

I Should Not Have Said That 61

Surprise, Surprise! 68

The Door of Death 71

Cat Toy 76

Fairy in a Bottle 83

Into the Depths 87

Time Loop of Terror 95

I Face My Fears 103

Close to Death 106

Back Here Again 110

Puppy! 116

We're Doomed! Or Not? 119

Mistakes Were Made 123

Gone Without A Trace 128
Snowball Fight 131
Revenge... 136
One-on-One.. 141
The Library 144
A Hidden Message Long Forgotten 149
Epilogue 160
About the Author... 161
The Lost Fairy Chronicles Book II: The Adventures of Wren D'laire.
.... 162

Prologue

The year is 2050. The world is in despair. People are starving. Crops are dying and animals are getting sick. Lakes and rivers, and even oceans, are drying up. Each storm lasts longer than the last. Natural disasters are destroying everything. The world is in chaos. Scientists have been laboring over projects for years, since before the new millennia. Their goal is to end the storms. If they can stop the devastating storms, then maybe they could stop everything else. Their newest and perhaps last hope is the StormChaser.

In concept, the StormChaser would capture and shrink storms, allowing scientists to contain the storms in capsules. This would end the vicious cycle. But for years, they have failed. One after another, either dying at the hands of the machine, giving up hope, or simply disappearing, the scientists came and went, but StormChaser never did what we needed it to save us. Then…I came along.

My name is Sage Amberly Hawkins, and I hope to finally bring the StormChaser to reality. At age 10, after seeing all the suffering in the world, I decided I wanted to study engineering. I made it my mission to work at Manna Labs and be a part of the solution. Everything was falling into place until…

The Interview

Six months earlier...

I am Sage Hawkins. I'm nineteen years old. Today I am interviewing for a position at Manna Science Labs, where I have always dreamed of working. I got a scholarship to go to college when I was sixteen.

Driven by my desire to make a difference, I studied incessantly so that I could graduate early. I finished college at the age of eighteen. I was the only one in my graduating class to finish in two years.

To say I am nervous would be an understatement; today is a very important day.

"Wake up, honey. It's your big day," my mom whispered.

My mom is the best. She always made my favorite breakfast on special occasions like today. Even though I am old enough to make my meals, she insists. I grew up fast, so she is probably hanging on to my childhood, and this is her way of showing it.

"Fine, fine," I said, yawning.

My mom left the room, shutting the door behind her. I got out of bed, brushed my hair, and put it in a braid. My hair was so tangled that I had to brush through it for five minutes to get the knots out. You'd think I was harboring an animal in there or something.

Putting on my favorite knee-length, dark-blue dress and matching pearl necklace, I went into my bathroom to brush my teeth. My hair wasn't in much better shape than before I'd brushed it, but it would have to do. With a wink, a smile, and a little twirl for good luck, I kiss my fingertips and patted them on my reflection in the mirror. *You've got this.*

Leaving my room, I walked down our curved staircase and sat in the kitchen while my mom made breakfast: French toast with a side of bacon, eggs, and a cup of milk to drink. It smelled delicious. My stomach was in knots thinking about my impending interview, but I was starved.

My mom set the food in front of me, and before I knew it, everything was gone.

"Thanks, Mom," I said. "I have to go if I want to make it to the interview on time. Bye!"

I grabbed my purse off the chair. It was black leather and had two neatly arranged pockets inside. They were closed by two small gold buttons. Purses like this one weren't seen much these days as leather became harder to come by due to the shortage of animals around the world.

"Bye, sweetie! Good luck. I know you'll get it!!"

I smiled and waved as I ran out of the door. We all smile these days, despite the sad state of things.

I hopped into my black 2030 Mazda3. It's old, but it gets me around. My parents say it's a nice car for its age. I checked my watch: 9:30. *I've got plenty of time*, I hoped. I blew out the nerves in a long sigh and pulled out of the driveway.

The Interview

After I left the subdivision, I merged onto the highway. To my utter dismay, there was a traffic jam. I honked the horn, groaned, and made a funny wish that people could teleport. So much for having plenty of time! By 10:15, I finally got off the highway and pulled onto Adams Boulevard. I was supposed to have my interview at ten o'clock. I was fifteen minutes late! My stomach churned. I willed the French toast not to come back and bite me.

Looming to my right was Manna Science Labs.

Taking a deep breath, I shook off my nerves best I could. They had come back in full force. The building was ten stories high and made of glass and stone. It was the tallest and fanciest building in town. Turning right, I pulled into the parking lot.

There were so many cars. Too many cars! People were walking in, rushing to start work. They wore the usual white lab coat and fancy I.D. cards. Each ID card had their names, Manna Station, and specialty. I even saw a woman I recognized from our neighborhood. She had lived across the street from us before she moved. Her tag read: Maddison Lee, Crop Rejuvenation, Production Specialist.

I stepped out of my car and hurried into the building, trying not to trip over my feet. Inside, the building was gorgeous. There were fountains everywhere, some spouting water five feet into the air. Lining the fountains were trees on all sides. The faint sound of birds singing could be heard over the whoosh and splash of the water. It all seemed so unreal among the chaos of the outside world. But here, at Manna Labs, anything is possible. At least that's what everyone's hope is hinged upon. Everyone who's anyone wants to work here. All of the top minds flock to Manna Labs. I was lucky to even be considered at my age, but my early graduation status, perfect grades, and application helped me stand out.

The floors were made of white marble and were polished so bright that I could see my reflection. My heart was pounding. My pulse was thrumming behind my eyes. I was already stressed about the interview and being late didn't help. I pulled out a small sheet of paper from my purse and read the room number. I didn't need to read it. I had memorized it the day that I got my interview. There was just something real about the piece of paper that I needed right then. It grounded me. I walked up the stairs to office 2098. A man was waiting for me there in the private meeting room.

I smiled. "Hello, my name is Sage Hawkins," I said cautiously, aware of my tardiness.

The man stared at me for a while, silence filling the room. "Hello, Sage. You're late," he said flatly.

I looked downward. "I'm sorry, sir. There was a traffic jam, and I—"

"My name is Leo O'Brian, and I will be conducting your interview. What experience do you have in this field?"

I thought about it for a moment. I didn't know how to answer at first, "I don't have a lot of traditional experience. At the University of Berkley, I was the top of my class, majoring in meteorology and engineering," I said, hoping that was what he wanted to hear. "I have studied vigorously to get here. I graduated high school at sixteen and college at eighteen. All I have ever wanted is to work at Manna Labs and make an impact. It's my dream to make a difference, and I have some very specific ideas on how we could bring the StormChaser to life."

I was rambling. I was nervous. I knew it, and he knew it. He spoke after what seemed like an eternity.

"You're quite young, and you were late to your interview, which does not help your cause.".

I didn't think he was supposed to comment on my age, but before I could think, I blurted out, "I'll accept any open role. It's my dream to work here at Manna Labs." Even if I have to start with cleaning restrooms to prove myself.

Leo mumbled something under his breath. He did that after every question I answered. The interview felt like it went on forever. He asked another twenty questions before he got to the final one. "Would you rather be aligned to the oceanic clean-up team or storm capture project?"

My dream has always been to make storm capturing a reality. It would be life changing. Recalling my first hurricane and the fear in my parent's eyes as they tried to keep our family safe. I remember reading about the work early scientists did on the project. Always making progress but never having a working ray gun for size containment. I knew I could do this. I knew I could help.

"Storm capture!" I replied, without hesitation.

Leo looked at me. Was that a smile?

"Please wait in the hall. I need to place a phone call."

I nodded eagerly, pushing open the door to walk outside. My stomach gurgled as I walked out. That French toast was trying to pay another visit.

While waiting, people walked by, talking about things they would do once they got off work. I tried not to look like I might throw up. Some girl rushed by on her phone, talking about a family emergency. I couldn't wait for the chance to be one of these people, one of these scientists walking by in a rush, off to save humanity. All in a day's work. But I didn't have the job just yet. I certainly wouldn't get it if I up-chucked in the hallway. That wouldn't do me any good at all.

Leo pushed open the door and smiled. I knew it was a smile! "You got the job, kid. But you have big shoes to fill. It won't take much for you to lose your place here. Plenty of others far more qualified than yourself would love to be where you are."

I stared at him, wide-eyed, jaw slack. In my head, I freaked out. Oh my god, Sage, you got the job! I can't believe this! Stay cool, I thought. "Thank you, sir," I said with forced calmness. "You won't regret this."

He handed me a lab coat and a sheet of paper. Scribbled on it were a room number and the project I would work on. Room 3960, StormChaser.

I stared at the paper. "Thank you, sir. I-I can't believe I get to work on the StormChaser."

Leo smiled. "Go on now. Get to work."

Leo left and went back into his office, leaving me to stew and sweat all by myself. I took a deep breath as my blood raced in excitement. I needed to calm down before I met my new co-workers. Once I was ready, I slid my lab coat on and walked to room 3960. I pushed open the door and walked in.

This is it. Everyone stopped what they were doing and looked at me. "Hi," I said, "My name is Sage Hawkins."

In the corner of the brilliant white room, a woman with a gray clipboard looked up and locked eyes with me. She walked over, clipboard still clutched in her arms. Looking me up and down with her bright blue eyes.

Finally, she said, "Hello, my name is Jacqueline. I'm your boss here in this lab. If you make a breakthrough or need to report to someone, report to me." She said, talking very fast.

"Sage… Sage… Sage, here it is. You're the new one Leo phoned me about?" Jacqueline flipped through her papers and found what she was looking for. Without waiting for me to reply, she continued. "Great! Your job is simple. All you have to do is look over the circuit boards and make sure they remain functional." She pulled another clipboard from behind her and handed it to me. "This is your schedule. I hope it suits you. I have to…

Sally! Don't put that there! Ugh, sorry, I have to go… Sally, whom you will probably meet later, is putting… Bryan! That screw will fall out, then we'll have a whole other set of issues! You can tell I'm very busy right now… but if you need anything, come to me." And with that, she left.

Looking down at my schedule and the circuit board blueprints, I took a ragged breath. I was biting off more than I could chew.

Days Blur Together

Days turned into weeks and weeks into months. My job was to fix the circuit boards as the programmers and designers changed the code and components for the machine. The work was repetitive but fulfilling. The StormChaser was a giant drone with a capture ray attached.

Nothing too impressive. Inside were wires and circuits. It wasn't as glorious as I had always thought it would be, but it was still incredible. The machine still wasn't working, but it improved daily. Every day, I clocked in, repeating the same process as the day before, but I learned something new each time; watching and waiting for my chance to share a significant breakthrough or idea with the team. Then one day wasn't like all the others.

We started up the StormChaser for test run 6473-B. The storm indicator lights were supposed to be green, but this time they were red. The drone began to make loud screeching noises and then sent out bright lightning-type flares. Disoriented and blinded by the strobing light, Noel accidentally bumped into the side of the StormChaser ray beam, which was used to capture and miniaturize the storms. The machine tilted and aimed directly where I stood. Time stood still. I knew what was going to happen.

I tried to run, but it was too late. The StormChaser sent out a blast of light. The ray hit me hard in the back. I fell to the ground, feeling like every bone in my body was being crushed repeatedly. The pain was too much for me to bear. But everything got worse when I thought it couldn't go on any longer. I felt like I was directly under the sun, its ten-thousand- degree heat beating down on me. My stomach seized in agony as if a sword were being plunged into it.

I closed my eyes as the pain overwhelmed me. And the next thing I knew, I was unconscious.

An Unexpected Meeting

When I woke up, I saw everything differently. My colleagues towered over me. I knew what had happened, but I just could not reconcile it.

This can't be happening! I can't be shrunk! What are my parents going to think of this?! How will they even know? I am TINY!

My co-workers were shouting.

"We have to find her!"

"If Leo finds out, he'll shut the project down!"

An Unexpected Meeting

"We promised him no more incidents like what happened to Dr. Felix when he exploded!"

"There is still a lawsuit from his family in processing..."

EXPLODED!? Did they just say exploded? Well, I guess I would rather be tiny than splattered on the walls. But still...

They were running around like cattle chased by a sheepdog.

"Sage?! Where are you?!"

Sally ran right toward me. I could see her vast sneakered foot coming down. I dove to the left and barely missed being squashed by her gigantic shoe. Before I could think, Bryan's foot was coming toward me. I rolled and rolled away. This was a living nightmare.

I ran as fast as I could. My only thoughts were to get out and get back to my family.

I hopped down the stairs, hoping my legs wouldn't crumple beneath me as I fell to the next step. I walked in someone's shadow and used them to help me get out the door.

After dodging all the dogs and birds trying to eat me, I finally reached the bus station. A girl and her mother sat on a bench, waiting for a bus to arrive. The little girl's backpack was lying open on the ground. I sprinted over to the bag and grabbed ahold of the zipper. When the bus finally came, the little girl and her mother climbed aboard.

I attempted to climb the window to see where I was, but I failed. I tried to relax, knowing the bus ride would take a while. Suddenly, I flew forward and was flung out of the backpack. I fell to the ground with a thump. Pain coursed through my right shoulder. An elderly lady started to walk down the aisle as I looked up. As fast as I could, I lept. I caught hold of her shoelaces and climb my way onto her shoe. She stepped off the bus, with me hanging on for dear life.

She walked for what felt like miles. With my arms and legs already aching from the fall, every task I had to do to get home was getting harder and harder. I was exhausted. To my utter relief, we were at the bus station right next to my house. I jumped off her shoe and ran as fast as possible to get home. I hopped up the stairs and knocked on the door, but no one came. I tried over and

An Unexpected Meeting

over again… still nothing. *This is no use. They can't hear me. Maybe they'll realize something is wrong when I don't come home today.*

I was about to give up when my dad opened the door. I don't know why, but it was probably not for me. He started to walk outside. I realized what was happening and that I'd better move so he wouldn't flatten me! I dodged his feet the best I could. *Is this day over yet?* Once I was out of the flattening zone, I tried to scream his name, but he didn't hear me.

Moments later, he went back inside with the mail. It was useless. I am tiny, and no one knows I even exist. I hopped off the porch and sat at the end of the driveway with my head in my hands and tears streaming down my face.

Reality hit as hard and fast as the wayward Storm Chaser blast had earlier. The only difference is I had recovered from that. This was something I didn't know if I'd ever be able to recover from. My parents were gone. Not literally. I could see them. I could hear them. But I would never touch them, or hug them, or kiss them again. My mom would never wake me up with her warm French toast. My dad would never take me hunting or help me with my car... they were gone. I was no more real to them than they were to me. *This can't be happening!*

I shook, my body battling my mind to reconcile the tear in reality that this crushing truth had ripped open inside of me. My chest tightened and I lost all sense of where I was or how I had gotten there. My breath became a whistling, strangled thing as I spiraled further into this dark place.

My life had changed in an instant. Everything I had hoped and dreamed for, was gone. Will my parents look for me? Will they know what happened? I remembered what I heard about Dr. Felix. My soul was crushed by the weight of how his family must feel and how mine would when they heard the news that I was gone.

Then I heard it. The sound of someone or... something yelling, "Sound the alarm!"

As suddenly as it happened, a throng of creatures flew toward me like a swarm of insects. I hate bugs, especially bees. Once the group had landed, I got a chance to get a good look at them, they were all small like me, but they had wings.

An Unexpected Meeting

Whew, at least they aren't bees. Dodged that bullet. One tiny human walked forward. She was just a tad bit taller than I was. She looked very stern. "Who are you?! Where are you from?!" she yelled.

I stood frozen in fear. The woman glared at me. She shook her head in distaste. "Start talking. You're either our enemy or our ally. Answer or my friends back here will attack."

Looking over her shoulder, I saw at least twenty small people staring daggers at me. *Now I am being confronted by an angry mob of...what? Bee people? Have I mentioned this had been a long day?*

Overwhelmed, exhausted, and not wanting to die, I sighed and told her what she wanted to hear. "My name is Sage Hawkins, I work— worked at Manna Labs. I was helping develop the StormChaser project when a fluke accident happened, and it shrank me."

The woman looked back at her people. They nodded or shrugged. That meant something, good or bad. The woman spun around to face me. "My name is Captain Jones. Follow me."

I looked around at all the people, wondering if they were friends or foes. After I realized I had no other options, I agreed to follow her.

The one who called herself "Captain Jones" led me to the front porch steps of my neighbor's house. The Gregorys were not the nicest neighbors. They thought very highly of themselves and never interacted with us much. In fact, I often imagined to myself that they must be aliens from another planet. Which would go along with all these tiny people I am currently surrounded by. In fact…where ARE these bee people taking me? I wondered. Maybe they aren't bee people after all, maybe these are people the Gregory's shrunk with some alien technology.

What I saw next was astounding.

An Unexpected Meeting

It was a network of tunnels. The main tunnel led to a vast room. The smell of food caught my attention; there was a whole table full, just waiting to be eaten. And after the day I had, I was starving…or maybe I was just feeling sick to my stomach. When I turned, I saw a beautiful wood-carved shelf of potions in glass vials. A small tube with drinking water dripped delicate droplets out slowly for easy collecting. The tube reached the ceiling and out through the top. I guessed it went up the side of the house so rainwater could be collected. It looked like…no, it was…the stem of a dandelion! A mini oven, where clay cups and glass vials were made, warmed the room. As I looked at Captain Jones, I was struck by something else… a closet full of wings! Ok, I am intrigued.

"Please follow me," she said sternly.

Jones was tough. Her posture was stiff, and she was a little rude. By the looks of things, she was a fighter, and I guessed she was a good one. Who are these people? What are they? Had they been shrunk too? Were these the old Manna Labs scientists? My head was spinning.

Captain Jones led me down another tunnel and showed me a room. "You'll stay here until our leader comes to see you."

Then she left, closing the door behind her. I heard a slight click as if the door were being locked. I jogged over and reached for the handle. I gave it a good push, but it didn't budge. I sighed and turned around, leaving the hope to escape behind me. I got an excellent chance to look at the room now that she was gone. There was a bathroom, a closet full of new clothes, and a comfy bed made of leaves.

I went over to the closet and selected a new outfit. It was green, the same color many of the others wore. It had a golden dragonfly on the chest and a green leaf armband. There was a feathered headpiece that went with the outfit as well! I had to get out of my lab coat and pink undershirt. It was too small and highly uncomfortable. When I was jumping down the stairs, my lab coat was ripped. It was now torn and tattered. Slipping it off was not easy because of my shoulder, but I did it. I heard people talking outside the door.

A feminine voice said, "Did you lock the door?"

There was a long silence, and then I heard it. "Yeah, I did. I didn't know if we could trust her."

Someone outside sighed. Slowly and silently, I walked over to the door and looked through the keyhole, I saw Captain Jones hand the other person a key. A dark shape squeezed into the small hole. I jumped back, hoping to avoid being caught spying on the strange people. I heard a click in the door, and the other person entered the room. She looked to be in her mid-forties. Her outfit was beautiful. Her hair was different shades of purple and pink, light purple flowers adorning the sides. She wore a necklace of silver chain with a dark blue gem hanging from it. Her dress was long, all the way to her ankles. Two pieces of purple silk hung from her arms and fell to her waist.

Her wings were magnificent. They were different shades of purple and lined with silver. "Hello, my name is Aurora. I am the leader of the fairies," she said in a soft voice. "You're small, like us, but also not like us."

S. Hoffman

"Like us? Who is 'us?' This morning. I had a job at Manna Labs. I was, er, am an adult. I was... big. Now I am what? A tiny person the size of what... a grain of rice?! Surely not. And you are fairies? Fairies are real? I thought you were bee people or something." Fairies can't possibly be real but the people standing in front of me are living proof. Was everything I knew a lie?

She chuckled, "'You don't think fairies are real, but you thought we could be bee people?" Her smile softened my tense posture.

I stared at her like she said something insane, and she did. She was the leader of the fairies? This must be a dream. No, a nightmare. Then I realized I had to respond to her.

"How do I know if I can trust you?" I asked.

Aurora sighed. "I know you've been through a lot, but please tell me what happened to you."

"I got hit by a machine that backfired inside a science lab," I said flatly, reaching over and grabbing my shoulder. "I had hoped to one day save the world from all of the destructive storms and chaos. But that's probably never going to happen now."

Aurora tensed for a brief moment, almost unnoticeable. Then she sighed. "Oh dear, you've had a day!" she said. "I never got your name. What is it?"

I let out a deep breath. She seemed nice enough and probably wouldn't try to kill me as so many other things had. "My name is Sage Hawkins."

"Does your shoulder hurt?" Aurora asked. "I can fix it."

I didn't know what she would do to fix it, but my shoulder burned with pain. "Okay, fix it," I said through clenched teeth. Aurora pulled a staff from behind her back. It appeared to be made from a birch tree. Sitting on top was a beautiful purple crystal.

She pointed the staff at my shoulder, and the pain vanished. "Wait, how did you? What did you just do?" I asked in shock. Was that magic? My head is spinning. First fairies are real and now magic is real too?

"Sage, you've had a long day. Can I talk to you about some more things in the morning over breakfast?" Aurora asked. I nodded, and Aurora left the room. Without another word, I lay on the bed and fell asleep, glad I was finally getting some rest.

A New Life

The following day, I sat up in bed feeling refreshed. While brushing my hair with an antique-looking comb I found on the dresser, I heard a light knock on the door. When I opened it, I saw Jones standing there waiting to escort me to breakfast. Jones led me outside the burrow and around the side of a nearby hedge to find a picnic table. Aurora was waiting for me.

After a deliciously warm breakfast, Aurora asked a question I was shocked to hear. "Sage, I know it's rather sudden. Would you like to join the fairies? We can give you wings and a home. I think it would be good for you. However, there is one thing you should know." She took a deep breath, "Once the wings are on, they can't come off."

Still in shock from seeing real magic yesterday, I whispered to Aurora. "I just miss my family," I said sadly "Will I ever get to see them again?" *I'm not sure I'm ready to change my life like this!*

Aurora thought about it for a minute and looked at me. "If a fairy comes with you, then you can sneak into your house and see them at night," she said, hesitantly.

I still don't know, I thought, but maybe... Maybe I should join them. But what about my family? "Can I have some time to think about all this?"

"Of course," she said. "Take all the time you need, but I wanted you to know we discussed it and felt it was best that you have a safe place to be and friends to turn to. We don't know what is in store for you or if you'll ever be... big again, and it is a very dangerous place out there for our kind."

A New Life

We finished breakfast, and I went back to my room. Overwhelmed by the sudden decision set before me. One day at a time, I thought. One day at a time.

###

The days passed in a haze. Some days were more cheery than others. I wanted to visit my parents, but without wings, I had to wait. The fairies tried their best to make me feel at home, but I still felt a bit like an outsider. The fairies I didn't know stared at me as I walked by, like an alien invader in their home. I enjoyed spending time in the garden and the food hall but felt too uncomfortable to venture further as the tunnels seemed immeasurable.

I often cried myself to sleep. Aurora and Captain Jones tried to comfort me, but they could never fill my parents' shoes. My mom and dad were always my cheerleaders. They supported me all through school and my aspirations of graduating early to work at Manna Labs. I wondered if they missed me.

###

Three weeks later...

"I'll join," I said timidly as I entered the room.

Aurora looked at me cheerfully, and it was evident that she was relieved that I had made up my mind. "Well then, follow me," she said. "We must get you a pair of wings. Or as I say, the wings must choose you."

"At least I am not gaining a stinger," I said, quite happy with my first attempt at levity since the incident.

Aurora chuckled and walked on.

I followed her down the hallways, and she led me into the main tunnel. We stopped in front of a closet full of wings. It was like an elegant, shining vending machine. Wings of all shapes and sizes and colors hovered and flitted about.

"This is Vestium Alas, our closet of wings!" Aurora turned to face the closet and said, "Well then, which one of you will it be?"

"Who are you talking to?" I asked, unable to take my eyes off the enchanting sight.

Suddenly, a pair of wings began to flutter, and a chill ran up my spine.

Official Member of the Fairies

The wings rushed out of the closet and hovered above me. Their emerald-green color cast shimmers on the walls around us.

An iridescent gold tint was strung throughout the delicate surface. It glimmered like the sun on a lake at dawn. Aurora spoke calmly like she had done this a thousand times. "Sage, I promise this won't hurt at all. I will place these on your back, and they will adhere to you." She gently placed the wings on my back, and a few seconds later, I felt a tingling sensation. As quick as it started, it stopped.

Aurora smiled, "It's done! The wings are on your back, and now you're one of us!"

"Is this how fairies are made?" I asked, confused, wondering how these people became small and where the wings came from.

"Not precisely," Aurora replied. "These are replacement wings for fairies who have had an accident or damaged the wings they are born with. Only I can remove, repair, and replace wings. In your case, I can grant you the gift of flight. Now, follow me outside, quickly. The work has just begun!" She led me out the front door of my new home.

My new home...that was hard to admit, even to myself.

"Go on, try to fly, or flutter your wings. All you have to do is feel the wings on your body and imagine that you're flying. Soon enough, you will be!"

She has to be kidding. Just think about flying, and I will fly? She knows I was a human before this moment, right? This kind of thing is not going to come easy to me.

I tried to do what she told me; I went up. I was flying! But I faltered.

Fearing I would die, I began to spiral to the ground. "Oh, for flying out loud," I quipped.

At the very last second, I gained control over my wings and flew around freely. "Whoohoo!" I lost all sense of everything that had happened to me. I flew past Aurora's head, making a buzzing sound and laughing to myself. Aurora let a considerable grin sweep across her face.

"Great job, Sage! Now, I'm going to leave you with Captain Jones so she can get you some weapons. I have to deal with the mess the cat made. Jones will explain who the cat is. I hope to see you soon!" She was already flying away when I realized what she had said.

"Weapons!? Cat?! Do you own one? And why weapons?!" I asked.

Aurora shook her head. "The cat is our enemy," she shouted back. "And we figured out years ago that living under a house with a cat living inside was a very bad idea. Especially when you are an inch tall." Then she was gone.

So that's how big I am...an inch?! As soon as she left, Captain Jones flew in, landing with a loud thump.

She wore a blue pirate coat with a white shirt tucked under it. She also wore a blue captain's hat with a white feather.

Jones turned toward me and said sternly, "If you want to defend yourself, follow me."

"Why do I need weapons?" I asked.

Jones looked at me and said, "Well, in case anything bad happens, you will need weapons to defend yourself."

"Defend myself against what exactly?" I asked.

Without another word, she walked away back towards the burrow. I just stood there, yelling and waving my hands in the air. "Defend myself against what?" I followed as fast as I could until we reached another corridor I hadn't noticed before. She walked inside, and I followed. What I saw left me stunned. Walls and walls of weapons. Everything from bows to daggers lined the room. I'm still not convinced this isn't a dream. Two seconds ago, I just flew for the first time. Now I am being told I have to fight? What am I defending myself against?!

"Go on...choose a few," Jones said.

This brought back memories, like the time when my father first taught me to use a bow or when he gave me a knife to carry around because I had barely survived a bandit attack; or when he took me to go hunting for boar for the first time. After all, the food was scarce. A tear welled up in the corner of my eye. I brushed it away, trying not to think of my dad.

I paced the walls, not knowing what to choose but then I saw three items that caught my eye. First, a recurve bow. It looked like it was carved out of tree roots and marked with a delicate design. Next, a wooden longbow drew my attention, it had a carving of a phoenix on the limbs from top to bottom. Finally, my favorite - a dagger worthy of a knight! The hilt had two dragon heads leading to elaborate swirls throughout the blade.

"The recurve bow, the longbow, and that dagger," I said, pointing to the wall.

She smiled and pulled my new weapons down. "Please take care of these. They're some of my favorites, too," Jones replied. She walked over and gave the weapons to me.

As we started walking, a thunderous roar caught us by surprise. And every wall began to tremble.

The Cat Attacks

Boulders and dust fell to the ground from the ceiling. "Hit the deck!" Captain Jones yelled to everyone in the corridor.

As I rushed to lie down, I heard a fairy yelling for help. "Captain Jones," I yelled over the noise of the falling rocks. "Someone needs help!"

She looked up at me and nodded. "Let's go!"

We stood up and ran down the tunnels. Turning right, then left, and all the while dodging falling boulders. We found what we were looking for. The source of the screaming.

Jones did not like what she saw. A fairy's wing was stuck under a boulder. Running over, we gripped the boulder tight and slowly lifted it. The fairy crawled out slowly.

"Oh, thank you!" he exclaimed "That was a first for me. I am normally faster than that, but the boulder caught me by surprise." We locked eyes for a brief moment before he scurried off.

"No problem," I said, but he didn't hear me over the pandemonium.

Captain Jones looked at me with worry in her eyes. "What's wrong?" I asked, wondering what was happening.

"The cat. She's attacking again. Her name is Nyx, but some of us call her Shadow Blade. She becomes invisible when she steps into a shadow, making it almost impossible to attack her. Now come on, we need to help them, fast!"

I nodded. We sprinted to the main room, grabbing potions as we went, and then ran into a hidden corridor where a catapult was mounted to a moving base. As we tried to exit, the cat stuck its paw through the door.

The Cat Attacks

"Hide!" Jones yelled.

I looked at her, questioning where I was supposed to hide. After a few seconds, I hid behind the closet of wings while Captain Jones hacked at the cat's paw with her sword until it recoiled.

"Come on, we need to help the other fairies!" Jones said.

We pushed the catapult outside and loaded it up with boulders. Jones lit the stones, and we launched them at the cat. The flaming rocks singed her fur and skin. Instead of sending her away, it just made her angrier. Nyx hissed in aggravation.

Jones yelled at me, "Load the catapult up with pollen-filled vials!" I looked around in confusion. "Which ones are they?"

Captain Jones rolled her eyes and pointed, "The yellow stained-glass ones!"

I nodded. "Got it!" Okay. The yellow stained-glass vials are full of pollen. I paused for a brief moment, wondering what other things they have stored in these jars. I loaded the vials of pollen into the catapult, aimed it at the cat, and fired. The vials struck true and exploded in the cat's face. The cat started to sneeze uncontrollably before fleeing the scene. The fairies cheered and cheered. Captain Jones flew over to me.

"Good job, kid," she said. "For a newbie with no training, you have one heck of an aim. I'm proud of you!" Jones turned toward the fairies and yelled, "Sage Hawkins defeated the cat for her first time! Give her a round of applause!"

Now I think I get what Jones meant by 'defend' myself.

All the fairies cheered, clapped, and whistled. We were all very tired, but we ran inside to celebrate. A celebration of my first victory.

Party Girl

The party was unlike any other. There was punch, snacks, and more food than I imagined fairies could eat. How did they get all of this? It was a massive display of food. After being the main attraction and eating more than my fair share I decided to take a break and sit down.

A fairy walked up to me. "Hi, I'm Alex...oh wait! We met earlier, you're the one who helped with the boulder," he said.

"Yep, that was me," I replied.

"I'm here to escort you to your new room.".

Alex was a little taller than me and maybe the same age, or a year or two older. He had dark brown hair. It was tousled and a little unkempt, but that was the look these days.

"Um… okay," I said, a bit confused that I was being moved to a new room. I got up and followed Alex down a cozy tunnel. We walked for what felt like forever. Finally, turning to the right, I saw pictures of fairies along the walls. They must be famous leaders, like Aurora, I thought.

Being caught up in my thoughts, I missed Alex's turn and ran into a wall. "Ow!" I said while rubbing my head. I turned around and made sure that no one had seen, and then had to run to catch up with him. I caught up, and I apologized for lagging behind through panting breaths. He smiled. His gaze lingered a little too long on my forehead. Gosh, I hope I don't have a mark. He showed me to a door.

"This is your new room," he said. "It's next to Captain Jones and Aurora's chambers. They said it would be best for you to stay close to their rooms, so you feel at home. We know this is a big change for you. Anyway…I hope you like it.

I opened the door and found the most excellent room I had ever seen.

There was a master bed made out of leaves. An adjoining bathroom was connected just across the room from the bed. For a bedroom that was underground, it had all the perks. But then again, I guess this is to be expected since this was the tunnel where all the leader's rooms were located.

Why would they put me in the tunnel where all the leaders' rooms are located?

The room had a beautiful armoire made of tree roots. I walked over to it and slowly opened the doors. Alex followed me into the room. Inside were many beautiful outfits, from armor for warriors to dresses for dancing. I pulled one out and walked into the bathroom, locking the door behind me. "One second, Alex. I need to change," I called through the closed door.

After I walked in, I could've sworn that I heard Alex say under his breath, "Ugh, girls... always want to try on new things..." I rolled my eyes in response even though he couldn't see my face. I'd change as fast as I could.

The outfit was green and had gold plates lined with emeralds and came with a pair of light green leggings, a dark green skirt, and brown leather ankle boots. It even had a light green cape. Oddly enough, it fit me perfectly. Had someone been expecting me? Before I walked out, I pulled my hair out of its braid. I looked in the mirror, hoping I looked okay. Opening the bathroom door, I walked out slowly. I stood in front of Alex and spun in a circle.

"So... what do you think?" I asked.

For a moment, he stared at me open-mouthed.

"What's wrong?" I asked. "Do I look okay? Is there something in my hair?" I started fiddling with the orange locks that draped across my shoulders.

"No, no, Sage," he said. "There is nothing in your hair, and you look fine. I was just... erm... well..."

I stopped messing around with my hair. "Well, come on now, don't be shy," I said. "Spit it out!"

He looked down at his feet for a while, and finally, he looked me in the eyes. "Well... that outfit looks really nice on you."

There was an awkward silence.

"Thank you," I said. "Well, I'm going to call it a night. See you in the morning?"

"Sure," Alex said, walking out of the room slowly. I collapsed into the bed in exhaustion. I think I fell asleep before my eyelids even closed, completely forgetting to change out of my new outfit. I was so tired. What a day!

You're Late

A distant sound woke me. It sounded like knocking. I got up and opened the door, yawning. Alex was standing there, waiting. No one spoke, and silence filled my room.

"Is there somewhere I have to be?" I asked.

"We're supposed to be at weapons training with Jones! We've got to go! We're late! Follow me, I know a shortcut!"

It's a good thing I'm still dressed, I thought. Alex was unfazed by my attire being the same as the night before.

Alex ran down a hallway and took a sharp right. I was right on his tail. Don't bump into a wall. Don't bump into a wall. He looked over his shoulder to see if I was still with him. He ran to the left, and before I knew it, there was the backside of a portrait hanging in front of us. Alex peered through a tiny hole. He beckoned me to scoot closer.

"Here, look through this," he whispered.

He moved to the side so I could look through the hole. I saw a massive room with twenty fairies inside. It appeared everyone was divided into two different sections, the first was for sword and dagger practice, and the next was an archery range. Jones had her back to us, which was the perfect chance to sneak through.

"Now's our chance," I whispered. "Let's try to sneak in!"

We moved the heavy portrait to the side. Trying not to let it slip and slam down, we squeezed through the small gap. But before we could get in line for practice, someone yelled, "What do you two think you're doing?"

Celebrity in a Day

Captain Jones strode confidently up to us. "You're late," Jones said flatly, expecting one of us to respond.

Man, she sure knows how to make you feel bad, I thought.

"Sorry, Captain Jones," Alex said. "I was going to wake Sage up to bring her here, but Alora needed my help with something, and it took longer than I thought it would…" he trailed off, realizing his excuses didn't mean that much to Jones. She takes her training sessions seriously.

Captain Jones nodded in dismissal. "Alex, I believe you know what station to go to first," she said.

"Yes, Captain Jones, sword and dagger station."

She nodded once more. "Go on now, get to work!" Alex ran off and laughed at something another boy said while he was sword fighting. Captain Jones snapped me out of my thoughts "I like your new outfit, Sage."

I nodded slowly "What? Oh, um, thanks," I mumbled. "It's nice to feel like one of the team."

"If you'd like to follow me," she said. "I'll show you to your station."

I nodded again, hoping I was going to archery first. Jones led me over to the range and explained the rules. Itching to show them what I could do, I listened intently.

"There are fifteen targets. Each one is farther away than the last," she explained. "The farther away the target, the more points you earn. If you miss a shot, you lose all your points, and you must start again. If that happens, go to the end of the line and await your turn."

The rules of this game sounded easy enough. I have been using a bow since I was quite young and haven't missed a shot since I learned how to hold a bow. My dad taught me well.

Captain Jones moved me to the front of the line. "Okay, you start shooting. I'm going to check on the sword and dagger station." She soon walked away and fussed over a girl's technique at the other station. I pulled an arrow out of the nearby quiver, grabbed the bow at the station, and knocked the arrow. I pulled the string back to the corner of my mouth. At first, I was aiming for the closest target, but then I aimed for the farthest. I pulled back on the string just a little bit more... then released.

My aim struck true, it hit the farthest target. Bull's eye! The room fell silent in an instant. Everyone in the archery station just stared for a moment and then cheered.

Across the room, I heard Alex and Captain Jones say, "why are they cheering?" Out of the corner of my eye, I saw them walking over. I smiled. It's time to show everyone what I can do. I knocked another arrow and released it. One after another, I let them fly. In rapid-fire succession, they all hit dead center on the furthest target. My final arrow split the shaft of the first arrow I'd sunk into the center circle. I turned around to see everyone in the room huddled around me, with their mouths wide open. "What?" I asked. Their eyes pressed in on me in shock. Alex and Jones arrived.

Jones broke the silence. "Sage, that was the best shooting I have ever seen. I want you on the Fairy Guard."

I looked at Jones. "What's the Fairy Guard?"

"It is an elite group of fairies that I train to be on lookout duty and in the front-line during battles."

"You want me?" I couldn't believe what I was hearing. She nodded as if hoping I would say yes. "Okay, sure," I said. Jones put her hand out, and I shook it proudly.

"Follow me, everyone!" she said. "It's time for breakfast!"

The mob of fairies gathered and followed Captain Jones, but Alex stayed behind. Once everyone left the room, Alex said, "That was some amazing shooting."

"Thanks, my dad trained me at a young age. I am lucky to have had him, he was…is… the best."

"I… um… I'd better go get some breakfast," he said. "Bye, Sage." And just like that, he walked out of the training room. I could tell he felt bad for bringing up a sore subject, but it was nice of him, nonetheless. Sliding the picture away, I left the training room for the food hall.

My Friend Has Freaky Powers

I tried to find the dining hall but got lost. Even after all those weeks, I still got turned around. The room seemed impossible to locate until a girl with black hair and gray eyes walked up to me. She was my height and looked friendly. She wore a gorgeous dress that appeared to be on fire. The dress was short in the front and long in the back. There was a leather waistband at her ribs, and in the middle of the waistband was cross stitching that held it together. She wore wristbands made of leather strips and ribbons and black high heels with gold swirls that were to die for. In her hair was a simple clip with a red flower.

When she got closer, I noticed something about her eyes: her irises were red and then faded out to gray. Her hair wasn't just black. The top of her hair was black, then it faded down into red, orange, and yellow. Her wings were yellow at the base, fading into orange and then red. And the very tips were on fire. A sight to behold...

"Hi, my name is Phenyx," she said. "I think you've met my brother, Alex. So, your Sage Hawkins, huh?"

"Yes," I said. Had Alex told her about me? "You wouldn't know the way to the dining hall, would you?"

She looked at me for a minute and then nodded. "I'm sorry. Of course, I'll take you. I was lost in my thoughts for a moment."

I smiled in thanks. She led me down the tunnel I had just walked through. We passed a photo I had not seen before, or at least I had not noticed it. It was a family portrait.

The young girl in the photo was Phenyx when she was younger, but the adults…I had not seen them in the burrow before. Alex was next to Phenyx, and the woman behind him had her hand on his shoulder.

I stopped, and Phenyx paced ahead, unaware I had fallen behind. "Phenyx?" I called out. "Who are these people with you and your brother?"

Phenyx walked back hesitantly.

Something changed in her for a moment. Glossy tears shadowed her eyes as she tried to hold them in.

"Those are our parents. They left about a year ago for a supply run but never returned. We have been living with our Aunt Kassie ever since." A tear rolled down her cheek, but she quickly brushed it away with the back of her hand. "It's not the same, but I know how you feel."

We both took a breath. A silent understanding passed between us.

Without another word, we continued down the tunnel. After several turns, Phenyx finally stopped in front of a door.

"Here we are," she said, still a little emotional from the earlier moment.

She pushed open the door. As always, hundreds of fairies were gathered over breakfast. Phenyx led me to the food counter. She walked ahead of me, got her food, and sat next to Alex at his table. I walked in and ordered my food. The food fairy handed me my plate, which included a bowl of fruit salad, a leaf cup of water, and a small loaf of bread.

"Thanks!" I smiled sweetly. I walked away to look for a table when Alex and Phenyx beckoned me over to theirs. I walked and sat down in front of Alex and Phenyx. This was the first time I felt like I belonged.

"So Sage, I heard about your amazing shooting in the training room," Phenyx said, urging me to answer.

"Well, I'm not that good..." I replied.

Alex looked at me. "Sage, don't be modest. You were phenomenal!" I looked into Phenyx's eyes, hesitant to talk about my parents again.

"My dad taught me how to shoot while living on our farm in Oregon. My dad and I would hunt for boar and deer. He taught me everything I know. He's a skilled marksman and was adamant that I learn for protection and food. It appears he was onto something," I chuckled.

"So, I guess you're good with the dagger you have at your hip?" Alex asked while glancing down to my side.

I nodded. "You got that much right. My dad always made me carry one around because of bandits. I was attacked once. I barely made it out of the fight alive. We moved here to California to get away from the riff raff." Alex and Phenyx were nodding their heads in understanding. I decided to break the silence. "Phenyx, why are your eyes that color?"

Alex looked at me wide-eyed. "Please, please, Sage, don't get her started!"

It was too late. "Well, you see, Sage, every five hundred years one, and only one, fairy will be born with special powers. And that happens to be me. Different fairies can have different powers. Mine... well, I'll show you."

She lit her hands on fire. The red part of her eyes glowed ever so slightly, blending in with the gray and forming the magnificent color of fire. Her dress glowed the color of fire too. As her hair flowed out behind her, it looked like it was floating in a light breeze. Sadly, the other fairies didn't like it as much. Everyone in the dining hall yelled.

"Phenyx! Don't do it here! You will catch something on fire like last time!"

"Everybody get down! She's doing it again!"

The warnings went on and on.

"Sorry," Phenyx whispered in a small voice. She cooled down her hands, her dress stopped glowing, her eyes returned to their normal color, and her hair stopped flowing behind her.

"Oh, Phenyx," I said, sighing. "That was magnificent!"

Alex rolled his eyes, clearly annoyed with the display, likely out of jealousy since he wasn't the chosen fairy with powers. Either way, it was incredible!

I Should Not Have Said That

Later that afternoon, Alex led me down the hallway to my bedroom. I thought we were lost yet again, but we suddenly appeared in front of my door. *Someday I will learn these halls.* I opened the door and went in. Once inside, I opened the door wider.

"Please come in," I said. I waited for his reply or motion of acceptance of my invitation. Alex smiled, walked in, and sat on my bed. "Alex, I need to ask you something… Will you come with me to visit my parents?" I didn't want to see my parents, but I felt I needed to.

He smiled. "Of course, I will."

Five hours later, we left the burrow and flew into my house through my parents' broken window. They had always planned to fix it but didn't. They were sleeping peacefully, but I knew they were probably worried about me.

I need a way to tell them I'm safe, but how?

I flew over to my mom's bedside table and found a scrap piece of paper and an extra small pencil my dad used for golf. I never did understand why they used tiny pencils for that game.

I wrote down everything. I told them about the accident, the fairies, where we lived, etc. I had no idea if they would be able to read my tiny writing on this scrap paper, but I had to try. I missed them desperately. I love my fairy friends, but these were my mom and dad! My parents! Once I was finished writing, I left the paper and pencil on mom's desk.

I flew up to Alex and said, "Ok. Let's go."

Alex turned toward the window. We flew back to the burrow. Alex once again led me to my room. He opened the door and let me in.

Before entering, Alex told me to get lots of rest because we were up so late. He left me to sleep and walked down the corridor. I shut the door. I changed into my pajamas, brushed my hair, walked over to my bed, and flopped down. After a while, I fell asleep, feeling better that I had left a note for my family.

I woke up to the sound of shouting coming from the halls and the smell of dust falling from the ceiling. I ran toward the sound. All the fairies in the burrow were gathering in the practice room. Jones and Aurora were standing in front of everyone. Jones looked through a periscope that I hadn't seen during practice. After looking through the scope for a while, Jones stepped away, and Aurora slid into her place. She only looked for a second and then scanned the crowd for someone. Me.

Aurora stared right at me. "Sage Hawkins! What have you done?!"

I stared wide-eyed. Oh no! The letter! I told my parents about fairies! What was I thinking? In my haste to tell my family that I was safe, I had put everyone in grave danger!

"Sage, what did you do?" Alex looked at me with his eyebrows raised.

I looked down in shame. "Now's not the time, Alex."

Aurora and Jones made their way through the crowd. Jones scanned everyone with a determined look in her eyes. "Alora, Alex, James, Mirabelle, come with me and plan for an attack." Aurora glared at me and then ignored me completely as she walked by, but Jones grabbed me by the arm and pulled me after her.

I looked back at Alex and mouthed, "Please help."

But this time, Alex looked at me helplessly and shook his head. I groaned while being dragged behind Jones. We met at the front of the burrow to listen in on the conversation.

"Our daughter is living under your porch!" My mother yelled. There was a long silence.

"Hahaha! You're so funny, Mrs. Hawkins! And no, I won't check for her under my porch. How would your child even fit under our porch?" He turned to walk away. "I know you miss her after the accident at Manna Labs but this is going too far."

My parents stormed away, fuming. As soon as they left, an eyeball looked into the burrow, and all the fairies, including me, stepped back. "Honey, call the pest control ASAP!"

The eye backed away, and Jones started giving orders. "Prepare to attack! We need oil and pollen. We can't let him see us, even if that means blinding him! Go now!"

Every fairy in the room rushed to the potion shelf, grabbed handfuls of the potions that Captain Jones requested, and flew outside.

We circled above Mr. Gregory and dropped our potions. "What the heck!?" he yelled when the oil hit him.

Next, we dropped the pollen, most of it landing in his eyes.

"I can't see!! No!"

He was so dramatic - we didn't blind him. The Gregorys had always been a little eccentric. They weren't my parent's favorite neighbors. I wasn't surprised he thinks he's blind.

Mrs. Gregory pulled her phone out of her pocket and tapped her finger against the screen, and the phone rang out loud.

"911, what's your emergency?" A female voice said out of the phone. "My husband just encountered hundreds of tiny people living under our house. They're attacking him! He can't see because they blinded him."

There was a long pause then the voice replied, "Okay, Ma'am. Tiny people? Sure… I am sending two police officers your way along with an ambulance."

One of the fairies tugged my wrist and mumbled, "We should leave before we get caught."

Back inside the Burrow, Jones and Aurora pulled me into a room. They chatted for quite some time, then Jones walked over to me, and what she said next lit my fuse. "We have to send in the MWT."

I opened my mouth to speak, but Jones cut me off. "Before you ask what the MWT is, I'll tell you. The MWT is a memory wipe team. We will have to erase any traces of you from your parents' minds. They won't know you exist. We also have to erase the memories of us from the Gregorys. They just left for the hospital. No one is going to believe them. More than likely, they will think he is delusional, and they will send him to therapy. No casualties today…thankfully. But that could have gone differently."

Tears began streaming down my face. I wasn't listening to the end of what Jones said. "But they are my only family, and you're saying they won't even know I'm their daughter?" I was crying. "You can't do this!"

They both shook their heads. "Sage, I'm sorry, it's the only way. It puts us all in danger. You included! We know you miss them and want them to know you are okay, but if you are going to continue to live with us as a fairy, you must realize your actions impact everyone in the Burrow! You should not have told your parents about the fairies."

Aurora shook her head sadly. Jones and Aurora both left the room. "Why, why me?" I cried, tears flowing like a river.

Surprise, Surprise!

A few hours after the whole "let's remove you from your parent's life" thing, Phenyx came to get me. "Aurora needs you in her office… and sorry about your parents, I hope you feel better soon." Phenyx gave me a hug to cheer me up. "I can't imagine what you're going through."

"Thanks, Phenyx," I said with a solemn voice. Knowing she did have an idea of how I was feeling. I stalked off to find Aurora.

Aurora's office was beautiful. There was a large oak desk and towering cabinets with glass doors, filled with books and what appeared to be loose paperwork on scraps of human paper. A crystal chandelier hung from the dirt-packed roof, and a bathroom door was squeezed into the corner of the room.

"Ah, Sage, you're here."

I just stared, not responding. My face was covered in dried tears, and the once happy glimmer in my eyes was gone. All that was left was sadness.

"Oh, Sage..." she said. "I'm sorry about your parents. But it's the only way. We erased the Gregorys' memories about us and then visited your parents. Is there anything we can—"

I cut her off. "There is nothing you can do for me. I no longer have parents! Who or what do I have now?"

Everything changed at that moment. Captain Jones waltzed into the room, her blonde hair swaying as she approached. I had never felt so unhappy to see her. She had overheard the conversation. She stared at me with her stormy blue eyes. But where the sternness should have been, there was something else... kindness? "You need a family, right?"

Jones and Aurora shared a look I didn't understand.

"Well, you see, Sage, we were thinking… Captain Jones or I could take you in," Aurora said. "However, you'd need to choose one of us to be your fairy… mentor? Fairy mother? I'm not sure what to call it, but we want you to feel at home here. We want you to know you're not alone. You are one of us now, even if it did happen in an… unconventional way." Aurora went on for some time, but I was too overwhelmed by everything to catch it all.

"I need time to think, thank you." I didn't wait for them to respond. I rushed out of the room with thoughts speeding through my head like a tornado had hit my brain.

The Door of Death

I guess I had to choose a mentor. This feels so strange. How do I decide which mentor is right for me? I wasn't in the right mental state to even think about this today. I just wanted to hug my mom.

Walking through the hall, thinking about everything, and looking at the photos on the walls to distract myself, I took a sudden turn, and before I knew it, I was walking down a corridor I had never seen before. It was dark and creepy, and it felt like something was waiting, just out of sight…

In front of me was a wooden door. It had one small round window; the edges of the glass were brown and rusted. The door handle was made of rusty metal too and had a small lock. Surrounding the door were vines wrapping around the top and reaching down to the floor on both sides.

Inside the vines was a single skeleton. The skeleton's mouth was wide open in horror. No key was visible in the area.

I shuddered. I wanted to walk away, but curiosity got the best of me. I slowly tip-toed toward the door. My hand reached out cautiously to grab the handle. I tried to open it, but it was locked. I searched the area again. There had to be a key somewhere. I looked around, high and low until I saw it.

There it was, inside the skeleton's mouth! I flew up and tried to grab the key.

It was heavy and made of brass. The last thing I saw was the bone designs on it. As I touched it, the mouth clamped down on me! The skeleton's mouth was slowly pushing down farther on my wrist. And soon enough, I heard a crack.

"Help!" I screamed in pain. "Please!"

The skeleton let go of my wrist, and I fell to the floor. Phenyx and Alex must have heard me scream, because the next thing I knew, they were there to tend to me, but as they did, the door opened. I stood up and tried to walk away, but something pulled me in. I turned around, and I saw a truly frightening sight.

There were ghost fairies made of blue fire beckoning me in. The force of their call was hard to resist. Despite the agonizing pain in my right arm, I reached my left hand toward the door. I almost fainted when I saw what happened. My hand became transparent like a ghost, just like the ones in the door! Next went my hip and then my shoulder. The weird thing was, it didn't hurt... there was a peaceful rush through my body. I looked at Phenyx and Alex.

"We have to get her out of here!" Phenyx yelled. The fairy graveyard is pulling her in! If she goes in completely, she will be lost forever!"

Despite the pain, I let them pull me out by my broken wrist. They pulled as hard as they could. I slowly backed out of the door. Before I knew it, I landed on the ground with a hard thump. I was lying on my back, groaning. Alex and Phenyx were at my side.

We all slowly and carefully sat up when the door creaked closed, seemingly on its own. With it closed, we laid back down, sighing in relief.

"Ugh, thank goodness that's over," Phenyx said dramatically. "The fairy graveyard almost had you. It's one of the last places remaining here in the burrow that Gwendolyn created."

Alex shot Phenyx a look and quickly changed the subject "Sage, there is going to be no rest around you."

I sat up, and Alex and Phenyx did the same.

I put the smallest amount of pressure on my hurt wrist and immediately withered back in pain, which erased from my mind the mention of someone named Gwendolyn and this creepy graveyard she created. The peaceful rush from the ghost fairies was gone, and the pain I now felt was very real.

"Here, let me help you with that." Alex pulled out a small jar of dust. He popped open the lid and sprinkled some on my hurt wrist. Instantly the pain went away.

"Thanks, Alex," I said, and then it hit me. "Ugh," I groaned, "I still have to tell them whom I chose!"

They looked at me curiously. "What do you mean by that?" they said in unison.

I groaned again. "A mentor. They want me to choose a mentor."

"Is that what you're thinking about after what we just experienced?" Alex exclaimed, clearly exasperated with me.

"Well," I said, "after all, I have been through… a fairy ghost graveyard behind an arm-eating skeleton door doesn't seem that bad." We all laughed. I breathed a sigh of relief. It felt good to laugh.

Cat Toy

I pushed open the door to Aurora's office quietly and peeked inside. Aurora and Jones took notice and invited me inside. I guess I wasn't that quiet. "I've made my decision." They both waited for a response. I took a deep breath. "I'm choosing... Captain Jones."

Aurora smiled. She didn't look mad at my choice, but Jones looked amazed. "Well, Sage, as my new mentee, I'm sending you on your first mission," Jones said. "We need provisions from the Gregory's house. We'll need some bread, vegetables, sugar, a few jars of milk, some cheese, fruit, and lastly, some nuts. Sound okay?"

I counted on my fingers how many things I needed to get. "Sounds good, but how am I supposed to carry all this stuff?"

Aurora's finger went up in the air, signaling that she knew something. She bent down and dug around for a while, and once or twice, I heard a few crashing sounds.

After digging, Aurora popped her head back up and gave me a small picnic basket. I grabbed it out of her hand and looked inside. There was hardly any room. I put my hand inside and tried to feel the bottom, but I felt nothing, so I looked inside. All I saw was a black void.

"I put a spell on it so you can fit almost anything inside," Aurora said. "We use it for these types of missions."

I nodded. That's pretty cool. "Am I going alone?"

"Alex has experience with provision runs. We typically send him," Jones said. "Phenyx, on the other hand... well, she may not be ideal even though I know you two are close. You choose whom you want to bring along, but you better go now before the family gets home."

I walked out of the room and waved goodbye.

"Sage, wait!" Jones called. "Take this in case of emergency, it will contact me if anything goes wrong, so I can come to get you."

I turned around and took the device from her. It appeared like it was made out of bits from human trash. The small device fit perfectly into my ear. "Thanks, I'd better get going."

Once more, I walked out the door. The hallway was deserted since most fairies don't go into the corridor where the leaders have their bed chambers. I needed to find Alex. I headed for the training room, figuring he would be there practicing. I snuck up on him from behind.

"Hi," I said.

He jumped back like he'd had a heart attack. "Sage, you scared me half to death! Please, don't do that ever again. You're lucky I didn't throw my blade at you."

Alex was breathing hard, and I could tell he got a good scare. "You're going on a mission with me," I said. "Get ready to leave." I lifted my picnic basket in the air.

Alex groaned dramatically. "Okay, fine," he said. "Just let me finish this real quick." Alex turned around and tried to practice, but I grabbed him by the wrist.

"We're leaving now," I said, making it a statement.

I dragged him out of the training room and to the burrow's entrance.

"Let's go." I took off out of the burrow, and I looked back to see if Alex was following.

"Who sent you on this mission anyway?" Alex asked, catching up with me.

"My 'mother' did," I replied, motioning air quotes around the word mother.

Alex looked at me curiously. "Your mother doesn't remember you. So, who are you talking about?"

Great, I thought. I have to explain the whole story. "Jones and Aurora offered to take me in. After… you know… the MWT took my real parents' memories. They are trying to make me feel better in their own way. They told me I could only choose one of them as my mentor." I tried to end the story there, but Alex wanted more.

"Whom did you choose?" he asked persistently.

"I chose Jones. But I don't want to talk about it anymore. Let's just go get the food."

Alex shrugged. We flew through the Gregory's keyhole on their door and into their kitchen.

"Okay, we need to look for bread, vegetables, sugar, milk, some cheese, and fruit, and the last thing we need is some nuts," I said. "Let's split up and look for the items. Oh! Here, take these." I flew off to the counter right after I handed Alex some small jars. I opened up a drawer and looked for some nuts.

Alex flew over to me in a rush. "Uh, Sage... turn around."

I turned to look at him, not where he was pointing behind me. "Why would I—"

He cut me off, and it probably saved my life. Alex grabbed me by the shoulders and turned me around. There was a giant shadow looming over us, and it had emerald-green eyes. The shadow stepped forward and flicked its tail. The tail struck an open mason jar that was sitting on the island counter and the glass container fell on us. In an instant, we were trapped inside of it. Nyx jumped down onto the floor. Her pupils got bigger, and she started to bat at the jar with her paws, shaking us both against the glass sides.

"This is not good!" Alex shouted. "I'm going to puke!"

Nyx continued to throw us back and forth.

"Just hang on!" I yelled. "Eventually, she is bound to knock the jar over."

"That could be the end of us!" Alex exclaimed.

"We can find a way to get past her, but first, we need to get out of this jar!" I replied as my head hit the glass. Suddenly, we felt the jar rock to the side, slowly tipping and preparing to topple. "Get to the bottom and hold on!" I yelled as the jar fell to its side. Nyx peered inside the jar. She put her paw inside and tried to grab us, claws outstretched. Then I remembered that I had my communicator with me! I pulled it out of the picnic basket and put it in my ear. "Captain Jones, can you hear me? We need help!"

Cat Toy

There was a long silence then I heard a response. "I'm on my way."

Fairy in a Bottle

Alex and I were seconds from falling apart, utterly exhausted from dodging the sharp claws of our feline foe. I somersaulted to the left and Alex to the right. Nyx peered in, giving us a short rest from her wicked claws. But not for long. She stuck her paw in, claws outstretched, and we veered to the side, rolling around like toys in a bottle. Her paw left the jar, and I fell to the ground, drained of all energy. It was getting hard to keep going. Alex kneeled next to me.

"We have to press on. We can use our weapons to save our energy," he said, pulling me up.

I grabbed my bow and knocked an arrow. I waited for Nyx to peer into the jar, then I shot. My arrow went into her ear. She shook her head and cried out in frustration, unable to dislodge the tiny projectile. Finally, she ran off. We walked out of the jar and flew off, leaving the food behind. We got halfway to the burrow when I fell out of the sky. I plummeted downward, with Alex right behind, trying to save me from the deadly fall. The ground was getting closer and closer. Finally, I landed inside a rose with a bounce.

"Ugh," I groaned. I was so tired that I could hardly move my wings. Alex reached me. "Can you fly?"

I shook my head. He put my arm over his shoulder and tried to fly, but we were both too tired to lift off the flower. We sat down on the rose, waiting for Jones to find us. I thought I was dreaming at first when I saw spots flying our way. But as I looked closer, I could see the fiery hair of Phenyx and the blue hat Jones always wore.

I tapped Alex on the shoulder. "Is it just me, or are Jones and Phenyx flying toward us?"

Alex turned to look at what I saw, and his eyes showed a glimmer of hope. "That's my sister, all right. You can see her hair from a mile away."

We stood up and waved our hands in the air. They flew toward us faster and faster until they reached the rose. Without needing an explanation, Phenyx came over and put my arm over her shoulder. Jones went over to Alex to do the same. They lifted us, and we flew back to the burrow two by two. On the way, we told them the story of what happened, including the horrors of being trapped inside a jar with Nyx on the outside. We didn't get the provisions Jones had entrusted me to get, but they understood why.

"We will send another provision scouting team out tomorrow," Jones said.

We made it back safely. Phenyx took me to my bedroom, and I assumed Jones did the same for Alex. Putting me down on my bed gently, she tucked me in. Bringing water to my bedside, Phenyx told me the story of when Nyx cornered her in the kitchen, almost taking her life before her Aunt Kassie stepped in and saved her. Exhausted, I yawned, and Phenyx told me to rest as my eyes began to droop.

I woke up to the sound of knocking. I grumbled to myself as I got out of bed. I walked over to the door. Opening it slowly, my eyes half open.

Despite it only being late afternoon, I felt like my body had just woken up in the middle of the night. "Hi, Aurora," I said softly. "What are you doing here?" I asked through a yawn.

"I was hoping to spend some time with you and show you something from our history," she said. "Phenyx is waiting for us. Why don't you get dressed, and we can take a walk."

Still half awake, I fumbled through the motions of getting dressed and wondered what was in store for me next. We left the room, the door shutting behind us with a click, and ventured into the endless maze of tunnels. Again, to somewhere I didn't know existed.

Into the Depths

Aurora was leading me deep into the burrow. Before we reached wherever she was taking me, the space began to tighten. The walls closed in on us, and the temperature dropped. We were going down.

We stopped, the walls opening up before us into a giant chamber in the middle was a massive tree. How can a tree survive this far under the surface, I wondered. I'll have to ask Aurora later.

The tree trunk was twisted. It looked like two flowers entangling their stems together. The branches spread out so far that I had to crane my neck to see all of them. Though the tree leaves looked like the ones on a willow, they were rose-colored. The most beautiful part was the hot pink blossoms sprouting from it.

"This is the Fairy Tree," Aurora said. "It's where all fairies were created. The blossoms are new fairies that will be born. Each blossom will choose a female fairy, and that blossom will give them a child. This tree has been alive for two thousand years. Its roots surround the entire burrow, forming most of the walls. We used to live under another house on this street, but rats invaded it, and we had to move the entire tree here... with the help of a bit of magic. We used to all be born with magic gifts, but then one day, the tree stopped blessing the newborn fairies, and now, only every five hundred years, a fairy is born with magic."

I walked up to the tree and touched its trunk. I looked back at Aurora, still touching the tree. "It's beautiful. How does it survive down here? Two thousand years?! "Wait... if you have magic, and Phenyx has magic, does that mean that you are five hundred years old?!" My questions felt endless. This was all such a revelation to hear and see. Taking it in was almost too much.

Aurora answered my questions one by one. First, explaining that fairies live much longer than humans and that, although the days are the same, they do not age in the same way a human would. The tree had been gifted to the fairies by beings called, The Ancients. Aurora spoke a bit about these beings and their role in the world's evolution but stopped short of telling me much more. I could sense a hesitancy in her, so I didn't press.

Aurora walked me around the side of the tree where Phenyx was sitting with a picnic dinner. After a long day and an incredible adventure - or two - this was a welcome treat. Phenyx brought out a bowl of salad, bread, and homemade butter that we passed around.

"This looks delicious. Did you make it yourself?" I asked.

Phenyx nodded proudly. "Yep, no one would guess, but I love cooking!" she said enthusiastically. "But Head Chef Fernando won't teach me more because of my fire powers. He is concerned I might light something on fire with my powers. I have better control over them now than I did a few years ago…but that's a story for another time."

The food was delicious, it was all gone in minutes. It was nice to have a quiet sit-down meal with Aurora and Phenyx. Meals in the dining hall could be chaotic.

"Sage, I believe you have to meet up with Jones to learn about the Fairy Guard. You're five minutes late," Aurora said. "Sorry for keeping you so long." She passed a piece of paper across the table. I grabbed it and looked at my schedule.

"The Training Room is close to your bedroom," Aurora said. "Go past Jones' room and walk four doors down. You should find the Training Room there. The Meeting Room is connected to it."

"Okay, got to go. Thanks for the wonderful meal and history lesson!" I ran out of the room.

It took me a few minutes to get to the training room. I walked in, and about a dozen or so fairies were practicing special techniques. They all stopped what they were doing and looked my way. A girl with cocoa brown hair and glowing brown skin walked up to me. She was taller than me by at least a pebble or two and wore a black shirt with a badge at the shoulder. The badge was yellow, with two swords crossing, making an X shape.

"Hi, you must be the new recruit. Sage, right?" She said with a light southern accent. I nodded in agreement. "My name is Aloralie. Call me Alora for short. I train fairies who will fight in close-quarter combat. Jones told me that you would be teaching the fairies archery." Alora paused. "Oh right, you're looking for Jones... um...If you go through that tunnel right there, you will find the Fairy Guard Meeting Room. Jones should be waiting for you there."

I smiled. "Thank you. I'll talk with Jones and be back before you know it."

As I started to walk away, she clapped her hands and yelled, "Back to work! If you're here for archery training, sit over there and wait for your new instructor."

I walked into the Meeting Room. There were handmade pillows everywhere, a few small couches, and one rope-hanging chair. Jones was sitting on a pillow, waiting for me.

"Hi Captain Jones, you asked for me? Sorry, I'm late…"

Jones turned around with a smile on her face. "Sage, hello," she said. "Let's get started, so the recruits aren't waiting much longer. You will be teaching the fairies in the Guard to use a bow. They are struggling right now, so let's hope you can improve them. I assume you've met Aloralie. She will make sure you're treated right, and she'll show you the ropes. Now, go get started."

I walked back into the Training Room and over to the fairies waiting for me. "Grab your bows and follow me," I said sternly. *I'm starting to sound like Jones. Oh, gods, I don't want to sound like Jones.*

My students grabbed their bows and got up. I walked over to the shooting range and turned around.

"Now, hit the closest target on the bull's eye!" I said.

None of them hit the target. I had a lot of work to do. I walked over to each fairy and told them how to do it. That they had to pull the string back to their mouths and hear a click when knocking the arrow. They must think about where they want the arrow to go, relax, and believe in themselves. My tactics worked. The first student hit the bull's eye. He stared in disbelief. All the other students began to mimic what he did. Eventually, most of the students hit the target.

"Good job," I said, proud of them. "Keep it up!"

We kept practicing for about an hour, and finally, I dismissed them to do whatever they pleased. Alora walked up to me.

"Good job, Sage," she said. "They didn't have a teacher, so I tried to teach them myself, but I think I made them worse," She chuckled. "They are looking good.

Before I know it, you'll be the next Captain of the Fairy Guard. Oh, and Jones wanted me to give this to you. It's your teacher's badge. See you tomorrow?"

"Sounds great. Assuming I can find this room again," I quipped.

Alora laughed, "It's a maze, isn't it?"

"It certainly is!"

She handed me the piece of fabric and left the room for whatever she had planned next.

"Okay…" I said to thin air. The badge was black with gold outlines. And in the middle was a golden bow with an arrow drawn back. I left the room too, ready to head to bed. I walked down the quiet halls, finally reaching my bedroom. I opened the door and went inside. I walked over to my dresser and picked out my PJs. They were light blue with purple metallic dragonflies. I changed slowly, enjoying the calm quiet of the evening. I put my hair in a braid and flopped down on the bed with a sigh. I was so tired that sleep enveloped me instantly. But sweet dreams did not await me, only nightmares.

Time Loop of Terror

A bright flash and I am blinded. Tears stream down my face. My parents don't remember me. I'm almost squashed by a giant foot.

Then everything goes still. One flash and I see it. As if in slow motion, a dazzling beam heading at me. A constant buzzing; in the background. People are yelling. There was an explosion of white light, then nothing. Just the blackness of a void. Then the day replays again like an infinite time loop of terror.

I jolted awake and sat up, sweat dripping down my face. My heart rate was unstable, increasing then decreasing like a blood pressure cuff was restricting my heart. My breathing was rugged and ragged. My lips were cracked and dry. That nightmarish time loop was all too real. All the horrible things that had happened to me this year replaying in grave detail. The feeling of being out of control was dreadful. Hopefully, this day gets better. I slowed my breathing and wiped my forehead. It was time to get up. Maybe a change of scenery would help.

I walked out of my room, hopeful for a day that would help me forget my night, but I should have known better.

I was walking down the hallway when Alora approached.

"How ya doin', Sage?" she asked, a hint of joy in her voice.

"Why are you so cheerful?" I asked, trying to hide my lousy night that was still lingering over my head.

"Today, I'm teachin' some new fairies who are joining the Guard," she said.

"Wow, that's amazing!"

Then the dreaded question came…"Did you sleep well last night?"

I had a quick flash of the cat looming over me and my parents at the Gregory's, not knowing I was there. My heart began to pound again, and I felt like I was going to choke. "G-get away from me!" I stammered.

Alora looked at me, concerned. "You okay, gal?" she asked, stepping towards me.

"I said get away from me!" I yelled, unable to tell the difference between my nightmares and reality.

Alora backed away from me slowly, putting her hands up in the air.

After she got far enough away, she ran off. I walked dazed to the Fairy Guard Training Room. When I walked in, I saw my students practicing. I tripped, and one of my students came to help me, but I waved him off. "Third target, bull's-eye, now!" I said loudly.

My students pulled an arrow out silently. They knocked their projectiles and released them. Most hit the target, and some didn't. I didn't scold them, I just let them keep going. I walked over to one of my students and adjusted her posture because her shoulder was drooping. Overall, the students did pretty well, a significant improvement from yesterday. But I still could not focus.

My mind was a blur after everything this morning. A pang of regret hit me as I thought of how I had treated Alora.

It wasn't even noon yet, but I was tapped out. "All right!" I said loudly. "It's time for lunch, class is dismissed!"

My students walked away mumbling about random things. Once they left, I began walking to my room, but my vision clouded like a wave washing over my body, pushing me to the ground. I tripped and fell, landing on my side. I looked down, and my ankle was bent the wrong way. Pain consumed me. I felt my ankle. It was broken, and no one was there to help me. I was going to have to wait for Alora to come to train her students. I scooted to the Meeting Room and sat on one of the couches.

Hours went by sitting on the couch, and no one came. I was in and out of consciousness as the pain enveloped my body. That's when I heard it. The faint sound of footsteps. Maybe they were here for training, or maybe they were going somewhere else. This was my chance to get help.

"If anyone's out there, please help me!" I yelled.

The footsteps stopped, and then they got louder until I saw two faces peek into the room. My vision was so blurry that I couldn't determine who the two fairies were. Whoever they were, they ran to me.

"Please help me," I said. "I need to get to the hospital for my ankle. Do we have one of those?" I'd never thought to ask before now.

They put my arms over their shoulders and carried me. We walked down a tunnel with many turns. There were hundreds of doors to go into, but we didn't go into a single one. The corridor led to a dead end with a single door. On that door, there was a plate with one word - Infirmary. They pushed open the door, and I saw the sterile room ahead of me. Fairies were lying on leaf beds. All of them were hurt. The fairies carrying me led me to an empty bed and put me down on it. They went to get a doctor. I never got their names, but they were life savers

The fairies came back with a woman in a white robe. She had cinnamon-colored hair and freckles all over her face. One of the fairies carrying me mentioned my ankle was broken. The doctor walked over and knelt. She felt my ankle, trying to see how bad the break was. I yelped in pain, and she stood up.

"My name is Charlotte, and I'm a specialist. I'm going to get a potion to help your ankle," she said.

"A specialist in what…?"

"Healing, I specialize in healing."

Charlotte walked over to a cabinet on the other side of the infirmary.

She opened it up and dug around for a few seconds. I had to force my eyes to stay open through the pain. Charlotte brought out a clear vial. She hurried back to me and unplugged the stopper. The liquid inside was the color of violet and very pretty.

"Drink this. It will fix your ankle," Charlotte said.

She handed me the vial. I grabbed it and swirled it around. It smelled like white chocolate raspberry cookies. I don't know how they do this - how they can make something as gross as medicine smell so magical. Oh yeah…magic…duh. I lowered the vial to my mouth and took a sip. It tasted amazing. Without hesitation, I finished the bottle. I handed it back to her, and she set it on a small table beside the bed. My pain decreased a little bit.

"I have a quick question," I said through a ragged breath. "I had a horrible nightmare last night, and today I have been having flashes of that same nightmare. Do you have anything to help with that?"

Charlotte's brow furrowed, and her look stayed like that for a while. "Sage...I wish I had a potion for that. For you to heal and your nightmares to stop haunting you, you must accept what happened. There is no potion for nightmares. Only acceptance and peace."

How did she know my name, I thought. Well, I guess every fairy in the burrow knows me, even if I don't know them, since I was once a human. I am a bit of an oddity. I nodded. "Okay, thank you." While listening to her, my heart stopped racing, and my breathing slowed. For the first time today, I was starting to feel a little like myself again.

Charlotte helped me stand up and handed me a pair of crutches. She assisted me to the door. "Your wound isn't healed fully, and it takes some time for that medicine to take hold so go easy on your ankle. One misstep, and you could end up much worse."

I waved goodbye when she pushed me out of the door. I limped to my room, hoping to take it easy for a while.

I Face My Fears

I hobbled into my room, shutting the door behind me. I spread out on my bed, closing my eyes. It took a while, but I fell into a restless sleep with no way out. Shadows lurked around everywhere, circling me. And so, the nightmares began.

The ground beneath me disappeared, and I plummeted downwards, not knowing if I would survive the fall. I landed on something soft but spiny. It was red and had bumps everywhere. It started closing in on me. Suddenly I realized where I was… I was in a mouth! A cat's mouth! With no weapons to defend myself, it swallowed me whole. I fell down a slimy tunnel, and before I knew it, I was at my parents' house. They didn't know I was standing in the room with them because... they had no faces! No eyes, no ears, no mouth, and no nose. Nothing!

The room shook, and a pit opened up below me. I fell in. I landed inside something that looked like the burrow, but there were webs everywhere. I wandered around, hoping I wasn't alone. Then I kind of wished I was. A creature loomed over me. It had eight long hairy legs, a round body, and numerous eyes. It was like staring into a funhouse mirror. Distorted and grotesque. It was a colossus... a colossus with fangs!

I backed up, running away from the arachnid. I ran through twists and turns, and then I saw it... daylight up ahead. I ran to the light. But the entrance was sticky. It was very hard to walk through. I forced my way in, only to wind up back in my house.

This time, I was looking through my parents' eyes. Running through their thoughts. I wasn't part of them, but someone else was. It left me in shock. My parents were thinking about a baby. A baby sister. Her name, Serenity, kept repeating in their thoughts. She was going to be born in December. It's July right now, so... five months. I'm going to be a big sister! I guess my mom was going to have a baby but didn't tell me. Maybe it was a surprise. My new sister will never know I exist. Maybe I could show up at night, wake her up, and talk to her sometime. But the one rule of being a fairy is no human contact. Maybe she would——

I jolted awake to the very familiar sound of pounding on the door. I slowly got up and walked to the door and opened it. Phenyx was at my door, with worry in her eyes.

"What is it now?" I asked. "I just woke up from surviving a nightmare. What's your deal?"

Phenyx could hardly speak, but she could say one name. "Nyx."

Close to Death

Phenyx and I rushed out of my bedroom to find fairies panicking and running everywhere. In the middle of the panic, Alex and Aurora tried to calm everyone down and told them to return to their rooms. We reached the others and tried to help calm the fairies. Of course, they didn't listen.

I thought I was hallucinating, but maybe I wasn't. I saw a figure forcing her way through the crowd, not because of fear, but with purpose. I tapped Alex and Phenyx on the shoulder. They spun around and squinted.

Alex nodded. "That's her, all right."

Jones ran up to us and grabbed Alex and me by the wrists. "We need you out on the field."

She dragged us along behind her.

Phenyx looked at me sadly. I just shrugged. Phenyx went back to trying to calm everyone down. Alex and I, on the other hand... I was sent to help the archers hidden in the trees, and Alex was sent to help the front line. I shot an arrow into the cat's paw, but she just hissed in anger. No matter how hard we tried, Nyx was winning.

I saw something that might help. I flew down to the ground and grabbed it. A box of human fireworks - Snapdragons! I reached down and picked one up carefully. It was heavy, oversized, and round. Slowly and cautiously, I walked over to the cat. She didn't see me because she was preoccupied with terrorizing the others. Alex was leading the front attack line. My archers were currently trying to peck the cat's eyes with arrows, so I just had to wait for the right moment. I ran and hid behind a stick, waiting for the right time to strike. It turns out watching a battle unfold can be pretty cool, as long as you're not the one being attacked or the one fighting.

I'm starting to get worried about Alex. What if he gets hurt? Or worse...

The battle went on for thirty minutes before I finally saw my shot.

Every fairy was lying in the grass, and Nyx was cleaning herself. I snuck out from behind the stick and walked around the great cat. She stopped cleaning herself and looked up. She saw me, and her gaze went from empty to full of anger. I kicked off the ground and flew up so I was level with her face. I looked at her with confidence. Flying in circles around her head, I lured her to the driveway. Once I was over to the driveway, Nyx started to jump. She made a sweeping motion with her paw, and I dodged it by just a hair. I dropped the Snapdragon, and it exploded at her feet. Nyx jumped back in fear, whimpered, and ran back home.

I flew back down to see all the fairies on the ground, standing up and waiting for me. But instead of cheering, they looked worried. Alex and Phenyx ran up to me.

"Sage, are you okay?!" Phenyx asked, panic-stricken.

I looked at her. "Of course, I'm fine. Why?"

Alex and Phenyx looked back and forth between each other, deciding who would break the silence. It was Alex who did it.

"Sage... your side," he said. Then I felt it, the throbbing, painful feeling that was engulfing my torso. I looked down, and what I saw made me swoon. There was a deep gash on my side, and blood was spilling to the ground every second I spent talking.

"What happened?" I collapsed and fell to the ground. The medical team rushed to my side and carried me away.

Back Here Again

I opened my eyes to find myself in the same room that I was healed in before, the infirmary. I couldn't remember how I got there. I looked to my left and saw a blank white curtain hanging from the ceiling. To my right, I saw Alex asleep in a chair. I tried to sit up but fell back with a yelp. Alex woke up.

"You're finally awake," he said while rubbing his eyes.

"Where's Phenyx?" I asked.

"She was watching over you a few hours ago, then she came and woke me up in the middle of the night saying that it was my turn because she had to burn your blood off the driveway, so the Gregorys wouldn't notice."

I nodded and tried to sit up again. Alex put his arms out to stop me. "Charlotte doesn't want you sitting up for a while," Alex said. "Your wound was so bad they had to give you stitches, and you're going to have to stay in one place for quite some time."

I groaned, pulling a pillow over my face.

"Don't worry, Sage," Alex said. "You'll be back on your feet in no time."

I glanced up, giving him a faint smile. "But my students, they need me!" I looked around frantically, trying to find a way to get out of this bed. Alex put his hands on my shoulders and gently pushed me back down.

"I've been teaching them," Alex said, trying to calm me down.

I stared at him, "No offense, but... you're horrible with a bow." Alex nodded in agreement. I laughed despite the pain it caused.

"How are they doing with their training?" I asked.

"They are doing just fine."

"How long have I been here?"

There was a very long silence. "You've been unconscious for two weeks."

I shook my head. "You're lying," I said. "That can't be true." I looked at him, waiting for him to respond.

"You've been here for that long, I'm sorry." Alex looked down, full of regret. "I should have pushed you out of the way when the cat attacked you."

I looked up to see Alex looking at me with sad eyes. I smiled cheerfully. "It's fine, really," I said. "The best part of being sick is that you can do whatever you want in bed. No rules!"

Alex brightened at that. Phenyx ran into the room, gasping for breath.

She looked at me cheerfully.

"Oh good, Sage, you're awake," she said, then looked at her brother. "You should have come to get me and tell me she was awake, you idiot!" Phenyx whacked Alex on the head with a small envelope. She rushed over to me and set the envelope in my hands. "It's from Aurora, Jones, Alora, and all your students."

I opened the letter. There were notes from every fairy I knew. I looked through all the papers inside. One of them read -

Sage, I hope you get better soon. Alex has been trying (more like failing) to teach your students. No matter how hard I tried to get him to let me teach them, he said he needed to do it as an apology. I don't know why he would need to apologize. It wasn't his fault that you got hurt. But he blames it on himself anyways. Please get well soon. - Alora

I handed the notes to Phenyx, "Put these on the bedside table, please."

Phenyx gently set them on the small table next to me. "So Sage, what will you do while you are here?" Phenyx asked.

I didn't know how to answer. "I... um... don't really know."

Phenyx smiled. "Well, thank goodness I brought these then." She reached into a small purse on her shoulder and pulled out some games. They were all like human games, one was like Chutes and Ladders, and another was similar to Candyland, but they were tiny.

"Did you make these?" Alex asked.

She nodded. "They are based on the human versions. After Sage joined the fairies, I thought that making a fairy version of Sage's human games would make her feel more at home. I have been waiting for the right time to give them to you," Phenyx passed the games to Alex, who passed them to me.

"Would you two mind helping me sit up, so we can play one of these?"

Phenyx went to the side with the curtain and grabbed me under the arm. Alex did the same on my other side. On three, they each pulled up and back and set me up into a comfortable position.

"Ah, that's better. Thanks," I said. I rubbed my hands together in anticipation. "So, which one are we playing first?"

Phenyx pulled out even more games and laid them on the bed for me to choose. Oh, how I love tic-tac-toe. So obviously, that's what I picked.

Phenyx and Alex were very bad at it. I beat Phenyx ten times, then she gave up, and Alex conceded after the first three rounds. Alex finally came over to play one more game with me, and I let him win that time. He thought that he had beaten me. Phenyx thought so, too. I winked at her, and she understood.

After a few more games, Charlotte came in and shooed my friends away, telling them that I needed to get some rest. Even though I was severely injured, those might have been the best games I've played in a long time. With big dreams of saving our planet driving me to grow up fast, I think I had forgotten how to just relax and have fun. Playing games with my new friends made the moment all the sweeter.

Puppy!

I woke up to the familiar sound of shaking. The walls trembled; dust fell from the ceiling. Nyx must be at it again. My eyes flicked open.

I wanted to get up, but I was still badly hurt. About thirty minutes after the shaking started, it stopped. And yes, I was keeping track. After all, I had nothing else to do. Soon, Alex ran into the room with Phenyx at his tail. They skidded to a stop, their shoes kicking up dust around them. They forced themselves to walk calmly the rest of the way.

"So how was Nyx?" I asked. "I just missed my chance to get revenge! All I want to do right now is slap the stupid cat in the face!"

Phenyx walked over, sat on the chair next to me, and put her hand on my shoulder. "Sage, we promise you can have a whole day to beat up Nyx once you get better. Sound okay?"

I nodded sadly, wishing I wasn't hurt. I sighed. Even my best friends could hardly cheer me up. I didn't know what could, but apparently, Phenyx did. Alex pushed a wheelchair made of oak leaves and branches into the room.

"Come on, we have a surprise for you," Alex said.

Phenyx helped me into it, then Alex wheeled me out. They wheeled me outside, around the Gregory's house, and into my old backyard. What they had there was cute and vicious. A three-week-old baby puppy was tethered down in my old backyard. Its eyes were a radiant blue, and it was wriggling around, making all kinds of excited noises. Its brown and gray fur was smoothed down. It seemed to be innocent enough. It was a Yorkshire Terrier. I had developed a healthy fear of cats. But puppies? They were special. The creature's tiny ears

Puppy!

flopped down to the side of its face. Its tail swished slowly back and forth.

I had a dog just like this one once before I began working at Manna Labs. His name was Milo, and he was the best dog in the world. He was so sweet. On my fourteenth birthday, he died of old age. Milo had been my best friend since I was born. This dog looked just like Milo, and it was making me cry. Phenyx took control of the wheelchair and wheeled me close to the dog's face. I stretched my arm and touched his silky-smooth fur, which warmed my heart.

"Hello Milo, I missed you," I whispered, leaning closer to snuggle with him. I looked over my shoulder. "Thank you both for bringing me here, but what are we going to do with Milo, and how did you catch him?" I asked, hoping they didn't hurt him to get him here.

As if they knew my thoughts, they shook their heads. That was when the shadow came. We were caught, off guard. My mom was looking over us! She was staring at the trapped puppy she had never seen before. The moment had suddenly become very complicated.

We're Doomed! Or Not?

Looking up, I saw my mother, but she didn't see me. Alex had tossed a camo blanket over my lap so I would blend in with the grass. She only saw the poor dog tethered down in my yard. My mother leaned down, untethered the puppy, and picked him up. She just stroked the dog for a while, looking around for ticks and fleas. My mom set the puppy back down and went inside. A moment later, she returned, looking for whoever tethered the poor thing down.

She walked around the yard, still looking, not realizing I would be squashed underneath her feet. Being in a wheelchair, I was in the most danger.

Alex and Phenyx were almost on the other side of the yard. They kicked off the ground and flew to me as fast as their wings would carry them. Sitting in my wheelchair, mom's foot was hovering over me, then just missed me by a thread. The ground let out a deep rumble.

Every second, the foot got closer. Her shoe was about to squish me again when Phenyx and Alex swooped in, grabbed the wheelchair handles, and ripped me out from under her foot. Mom's shoe crunched down on the ground. I took a deep breath and spun around to face an out-of-breath Phenyx and Alex.

"You cut it awfully close," I said.

They both looked down in shame. Phenyx was rubbing the back of her wing.

"Phenyx, are you okay?" Alex asked, setting a hand on her shoulder.

"I think that flying so hard, I must have sprained my wing." Phenyx made a small flame in her hands and rubbed it on her injured wing.

I guess fire heals her?

"So, will you answer my question?" I asked, "Where did you get the dog?"

Phenyx looked at Alex and nodded.

"The poor thing was stuck in your parents' rose bush. We just got the puppy out and had a bunch of fairies help us carry it into your backyard. Then they helped us tether the poor thing down," Alex said. "Also, why did you call him Milo?"

"Did I really say that?" I asked quietly.

They both nodded. I sighed, wishing that I didn't have to explain everything.

"Okay, look," I said. "I had an older dog named Milo, and he looked just like that. He died of old age on my fourteenth birthday. It broke my heart, and I haven't been the same since."

A tear rolled down my cheek, and then, even more, came pouring down my face. Alex and Phenyx both came over to me and gave me a big hug. I looked down and cried. We sat for quite a while, then I realized that Charlotte would be looking for me by now.

"Uh, guys," I said. "Charlotte is probably looking for me."

Phenyx and Alex's heads shot up. They looked at each other and rushed to move my wheelchair, but it was stuck in a drop of mud. They tried to pull me out, but it was too late.

A voice behind us boomed, "What do you think you're doing?!"

Mistakes Were Made

Phenyx and Alex whipped around and I groaned. "Hello? Anyone?! Is anyone going to turn me around? I would like to see what's happening." I exclaimed, annoyed.

They flipped me around, and all I saw was Charlotte's fuming face. "Oh no…" I said.

Charlotte flew over to us, pulled my wheelchair out of the mud, and rushed me back to the infirmary. I looked back to see Alex and Phenyx following, shoulders hunched. Charlotte rushed me inside and put me down carefully on the bed. Charlotte left me alone in the room and went back outside. A few minutes later, Charlotte returned, dragging Phenyx and Alex by the wrist. She shut the curtain to my room and spoke with Phenyx and Alex. Her voice was less than pleased. I heard most of what they were saying, even though I was not supposed to.

Charlotte said, "Why would you take her out there?!" There was a very long silence.

"We were just showing Sage a surprise," Phenyx said. That didn't cut it for Charlotte.

"But you should have asked first! Let me remind you, she has three bruised ribs and a giant gash in her side!" She yelled.

I saw Alex's shadow look down as Phenyx walked forward.

"Uh, Charlotte,'' Phenyx asked, "I have a sprained wing. Do you think you can fix it?" Phenyx was rubbing her lousy wing.

"Ugh," Charlotte said. "Fine, but you must promise not to take Sage out again. Got it?"

"Got it," they repeated.

Charlotte grunted, and speed-walked to the other side of the room.

Phenyx and Alex both sighed in relief. She returned with a small bottle and poured it on Phenyx's wing.

Phenyx yelped in pain. "What was that!? It burns!"

Charlotte nodded. "The pain proves that it is working. It will be gone right about... now."

The comfort was evident on Phenyx's face. Charlotte ushered Phenyx and Alex out of the infirmary. When she came back, she slid open my curtain and gave me my dose of medicine. It tasted like strawberries covered in chocolate. I really liked it. Charlotte fussed over me for the next hour, never giving me time to sleep. When she finally did, it was midnight, and I was exhausted. The weeks flew by faster than I could have thought. Slowly, my wound was getting better. Then one day, Charlotte gave me some good news. She nudged me awake at five o'clock in the morning.

"Wake up, sunshine," she said, setting a plate of pancakes next to me. "You get to leave the infirmary today. Now, if you feel any pain in your side, you need to let me have a look. And take it easy. Healing potions work, but your injuries were severe. It's taken a while to heal your wounds. Let's not repeat that. On the plus side, the last two weeks of rest and healing potions, also fixed up the rest of your ankle that needed to heal"

Charlotte helped me sit up, then she handed me a pair of crutches. *I've hardly had time to eat my pancakes, and now you're giving me crutches again*? I waved my hand at her, sat down again, and shoved some pancakes in my mouth. Once I was done, I picked up my crutches and left the infirmary. I hoped that was the last I'd ever see of that room again and hopefully the last time I have to use crutches. I had spent a month there healing after two weeks of being asleep, I never wanted to be there again. I limped down the hallway and into the Fairy Guard Training Room. I saw Alex teaching my students and Alora teaching hers.

My students were doing well, even though Alex was teaching them. He has always struggled with the bow. Alora was doing her usual routine with her students, making them run laps around the room. I snuck into the training room without being seen. I watched them train, train, and train.

Once they were done, I clapped my hands and slowly stood up. They all turned, and their jaws dropped.

Gone Without A Trace

"Sage?!" Alora asked, rushing to hug me. She wrapped her arms around me tightly.

"Ow, ow, ow," I said in a small voice. Alex came over and peeled Alora's arms off me, then hugged me, as well.

"Thank gods you're back! I was getting tired of teaching your students. I want to work with my sword again," Alex whispered, and I nodded, laughing.

"Okay, I'll take over again. But first, I would like to go to the main tunnel to grab something."

Alora nodded and helped me into the main tunnel. The other day, I was pretending to sleep when Charlotte told someone about a green bottle with a purple stopper and how medicine inside would heal wounds the minute after you drank it. I walked over to the potion shelf, looking for a green bottle with a purple stopper. I found every color stopper but purple and every other bottle but the one I was looking for. There was only one other place to look.

I limped over to the Vestium Alas and opened it. Inside were at least ten new sets of wings. But there was nothing else inside. I ran my hand along two of the walls, but there was nothing. I had one more wall to check. I moved the pair of fluttering wings and rubbed my hand along the back wall. My fingernail slipped into a small crack. I gripped the board and pulled. The board popped out into my hand, and sitting on the shelf inside, was the bottle I was looking for.

When I was in the infirmary, I asked Charlotte about it, and she said all it takes is one little sip, and your wound would be healed. I gently took the bottle out, pulled on the stopper, and took a small sip. Nothing happened.

I felt it at last. I felt like I was drowning. I felt like I was running out of air. Then it stopped. I looked down, and my wound was just a tiny scar. Then it hit me again. I felt like I was burning from the inside. The pain was unbearable. The pain stayed there for what felt like an eternity. Then it slowly dispersed. The pain in my ribs vanished without a trace.

How do fairies survive drinking this?!

I put the bottle back inside its hiding spot in case I ever needed it again. Now I understand why Charlotte didn't want to tell me about it. The pain is unbearable! I dropped my crutches, took a step forward, and staggered. One small step after another, I started to walk and then run. I giggled in relief. I had almost forgotten what walking felt like. I jogged outside, where Alex and Phenyx waited for me. Phenyx rushed over to me and tried to help me walk. I waved her off, and she did as she was told.

"So, what should we do first?" I asked. "I feel like I've missed a lot."

Snowball Fight

I woke up at least three times in the middle of the night, and it was ice cold every time. When I finally woke up in the morning, water dripped from the ceiling, and after it hit the ground, it froze. I groaned and got out of bed to go get Phenyx.

I found her where I usually found her, asleep on a lounge chair in the corner of her room. The door creaked as I opened it, and I let it.

I wanted Phenyx to wake up. I needed her to wake up. I didn't know why there was water dripping from the ceiling or why it was so cold that it froze when it touched the ground, but Phenyx might be able to solve it. I walked inside loudly, not caring to shut the door. I came over to Phenyx's bed and shook her awake. It took way longer than it should have. But when she awoke, she almost singed my hair off! With her hands on fire and at the ready, she blasted a fireball and missed me by a thread. Phenyx finally saw me, and the fire in her hands went out.

"Who did you think I was?" I asked. "A monster?"

Phenyx shook her head. "Worse, I thought you were my brother," she said, rolling her eyes. "Or even worse than that... maybe you were Gwendolyn." Phenyx suddenly realized something and put her hand over her mouth. She didn't want me to know about this Gwendolyn person.

"Who's Gwendolyn?" I asked, eyebrows raised. "You've mentioned the name before."

Phenyx looked at me for a moment, not responding. "Anyways... why did you wake me up? I was having a perfectly good dream about—"

"Got any fire hands to go around?" I interjected. "Please tell me, why is it suddenly ice cold in the burrow?! I would like some heat in this frigid place!"

Phenyx just shrugged, got out of bed, and followed me to the front of the burrow. We walked out the entrance and into thick snow. Phenyx lit up her hands, and the snow melted around us.

"Ugh!" I yelled. "It's September, and it's snowing! By the looks of it, the snow is over five inches deep! The world just hates me, doesn't it? First a near-fatal wound, and then five-inch-deep snow! Ugh!"

I grabbed a small snowball and tossed it at the cloudy, dark-gray sky.

Then it came to me. I spun around to face Phenyx.

"Have you ever had a snowball fight before?" I asked.

Phenyx shook her head. "I've heard of them but never been in one." I grinned and ran inside, leaving her alone outside. I went back to Phenyx's room and grabbed her coat, gloves, boots, and scarf. I ran into my room, grabbed the same things, and then rushed back outside. I tossed Phenyx her clothes as I put mine on. I slid my coat over my shoulders, put my hands in my gloves, wrapped my scarf around my neck, and put my boots on.

Snowball Fight

Before Phenyx could finish putting her things on, I scooped up some snow, pounded it into a small ball, and tossed it at her. It hit her in the middle of her stomach. She gasped for air and gave me a shocked look. She bent down in the snow and came up with an arm full of snowballs. She tossed three at me, back-to-back. I dodged the first two, but the third one hit me on my right thigh. I tossed another at Phenyx, and she burned it before it hit her.

Before I knew it, two hours had passed, and Phenyx was playing like a pro. More and more fairies joined us in the game. Phenyx, of course, was winning with her fire hands. Captain Jones and Alex came and joined us at about ten o'clock. After a while, Aurora hosted a party inside the burrow for the first snow of the year, and everyone gathered inside.

I got kind of tired of the party, so I went and stood outside to watch the snow. I had seen snow before, many times. My dad always took me hunting in the winter. But, I had never experienced snow as a fairy! The frigid fractals of the flakes stood out in brilliant patterns. Each one was enormous and melted on impact, soaking me in the process. I couldn't help but imagine the devastation one would cause if it was solid and frozen. I giggled to myself thinking about a million beautiful snowflakes the size of frisbees whirling around like throwing stars.

Another thing that I was not prepared for was how quickly I got cold. Standing one inch tall with paper-thin wings, now dripping wet, was a surefire way to wind up catching pneumonia. At least, that's what my mom would have said. Tears began to well in my eyes but quickly froze, catching in my lashes. I blinked them away, quickly, as I heard footsteps approaching. I turned to see Alex coming toward me.

"What are you doing out here?" he asked.

"I was getting tired of the party," I said, holding my coat tighter around me.

"Come on, let's go back inside. It's getting colder." I don't remember the last time it was chilly like this. I shrugged and walked back inside. Alex was still out there, taking his time walking in, enjoying the weather. After all, we don't see snow anymore. The heat and intense storms have become the only weather we are used to so this was a nice surprise. I wonder if the fairies remember what it was like when snow came every year…

Revenge

One week has passed since the snow. The fall weather was back. Which I wish meant it was cooling off but fall these days still meant heat and sun. However, the burrow being underground, stays cool and it turns out that we have a pool in the burrow! Alex promised he would show me. I changed into a swimsuit that Phenyx lent me. It had Hawaiian flowers and tropical fruits on it.

I stood outside my room waiting for Alex to get me. I pulled my hair out of its regular braid. It fell over my shoulders, very curly. I waited three minutes in the hallway, then Phenyx and Alex arrived.

"I didn't know you liked to swim, Phenyx, or that you were even coming," I said.

She shrugged, "I like many things. Swimming is one of them." Alex nodded as if to tell me that she really liked swimming. "So, are we going to the pool?"

The only response I got was an earthquake. I groaned.

"Oh, come on! For once, will Nyx give me a break? I mean, I just got dressed to swim! Well, I'm going to go get changed, and then I will prove that this cat can't mess with me anymore!"

I burst through my bedroom door, slamming it shut behind me. I slipped into my everyday clothes. I buckled my dagger sheath to my waist, attached my quiver to my back, put on my ankle-high leather boots, and grabbed my bows. The first one I grabbed was the recurve and slung it over my back. Next, I grabbed my longbow and clutched it tightly in my hand. I walked over to my closet and grabbed my arrows. I had twenty-four of them. Slipping them into my quiver and ran out the door to the burrow's entrance.

The cat, as usual, was trying to kill my friends. She was standing in the middle of the yard with my friends and a couple more fairies fighting next to them.

I walked out and flew up to the roof of the Gregorys. I landed next to my students and gave them commands. I drew an arrow and knocked it. "On the count of three, release your arrows! Try to get them wedged between her toes! One... Two... Three! Fire!"

A volley of arrows touched the clouds and hissed through the air. My arrow, along with many others, wedged between Nyx's toes. She hissed in pain and limped to attack more fairies. I spun around to face my students.

"Okay, listen up," I said. "I need you to keep firing at her feet, eyes, and nose. I have to go help Alora at the front line, got it?"

They nodded, and I knew I could trust them with this task. I flew down to Alora with my dagger at the ready.

"So, do I get to kill anything?" I asked. "Because I would like some revenge."

Alora spun around smiling. She came over to me and patted me on the shoulder. "You can't kill anything yet, sorry. But you can help us make this cat afraid of us. Just because we're small doesn't mean she can pick on us."

I nodded.

"So, where do you want me on the battlefield?"

She pointed to Nyx's right side. "We're low on fairies there. If you could go help them, that would be great."

I flashed her a grin and flew off to go help.

One-on-One

Alora was right. We were very low on fairies on the right side. Phenyx, Alex, and three other fairies I didn't know were the only people there. They were worn out. I landed next to Phenyx and drew my dagger.

"By the Ancients! You're here, Sage! We need a good fighter like you. Attack from the left. Alex and I will go from the right. I'll hoot like an owl when it's time to attack."

"Got it," I replied.

I flew to Nyx's left side and stood waiting for the signal from Phenyx. A few seconds later, I heard the sound of an owl hooting, and I charged.

Phenyx, Alex, and I met in front of Nyx. Phenyx lit her hands on fire, Alex drew his sword, and I knocked an arrow. I aimed for Nyx's eye, Alex for her paw, and Phenyx for her chest. Phenyx tossed three fireballs, and they burned into the cat's fur. Alex ran up to Nyx, cut off some of her fur, and gave her a minor wound. As she flicked her head around to look at Alex, I released my arrow, and it struck her eye. She hissed in pain after all our attacks. She swept her paw, and I dodged it, but Phenyx and Alex weren't so lucky. They didn't dodge fast enough. They were hit by the back of her paw and were thrown across the Gregory's yard. They hit a tree trunk hard, and their bodies went limp.

I spun around and gave Nyx a look of hatred. "Don't you dare hurt my friends." Pulling out a small bottle of oil and a bottle of trapped fire, I unsheathed my dagger and held it up. I poured the oil on it and broke the trapped fire vial over my blade. My dagger lit, and flames danced across its length. With confidence, I walked to confront Nyx.

Kicking off the ground, I flew up, leveling at her face. I pushed the dagger closer, and she took a step back. Circling her, I cut her in many places: behind her ear, on her nose, and on one of her paws. The flames from my dagger licked her skin and singed her fur.

I took a small blue vial out of my pocket and pulled out the stopper.

Inside was some water. Dumping it on my dagger, the flames went out. Next, I pulled out an icy blue bottle with a clear stopper. I poured the potion on my dagger, and the metal blade was surrounded by magical ice. I flew at Nyx so fast that she didn't have time to think. I made a small slash with my dagger. Her right front paw froze, and she limped back home.

I did wonder how the Gregorys were going to deal with this. I watched until Nyx went inside her home, then I heard screams of horror. A grin spread across my face, but it soon vanished. Alex was standing up, helping Phenyx walk.

Gasping, I rushed over to find out that Phenyx had one broken wing and a broken leg. With help from a few other fairies, Alex and I rushed Phenyx to the infirmary.

The Library

Phenyx was asleep in the infirmary, healing for the next few days. Alex dragged me out of there, saying I spent too much time caring for Phenyx. He sent me back to my room, so I could relax.

He said that he could care for his sister. I finally gave up and returned to my room to find something to do, but I couldn't sit still. I grabbed my dagger and bows and went to the training room, thinking that I would be able to relax there. I went to the sword and dagger station and practiced. I did a series of moves - uppercut, downward slash, and parry. Thirty minutes later, I switched to the bow station and ran through the exercises I taught my students. After a long practice, sweat was dripping down my back. I was out of breath.

Trudging over to a small bench, I grabbed the water that was waiting for me. I picked it up and gulped it down. I let out a deep breath and sat down, wondering what to do next. I heard the faint sound of footsteps entering the room. I waited and waited to see if someone would say anything, too tired to look up. The footsteps stopped in front of me, and I lifted my head. Standing in front of me was a little girl. She had light blond hair, milk-chocolate brown eyes, and sky-blue wings. She looked to be about five years old. She still had that childish face about her.

"Hi... my name is Willow," she said quietly.

I waved. "Hello, Willow."

"I was wondering if you'd want to do some crafts with me?" Willow asked, looking down shyly.

I nodded, smiling. "Sure."

I stood up and followed her. She led me to her room. Inside were long pieces of fabric. They went from each corner of the room to the next. She had a small leaf bed and a dresser. On her bed was a small teddy bear made of yarn. Willow led me to a blank wall and pushed on it. The wall spun us around, and we were in a different room. The room was filled with art supplies: clay, homemade paint brushes, paint, and so many other cool trinkets. In the middle of the room was a small table for two. I pulled out a chair and sat down across from Willow. She leaned down and pulled a small mound of clay from underneath the table. She gripped it tight, and it slowly split into two. Willow handed me a piece.

"Make whatever comes to you," she said while starting on her sculpture.

I knew exactly what I wanted to make.

"So, Willow, what's your favorite food?" I asked, forming the face of my project.

"Fruit salad," she replied.

There was a slight creaking noise and the sound of footsteps. I turned to see Alex standing in front of Willow's secret door.

"So, Willow, I see you've shown Sage your secret getaway."

Willow nodded. I looked from Willow to Alex. "How do you know each other?" I asked.

"I have been Willow's friend since she was born. She's also my cousin," Alex said, chuckling.

I nodded. "That explains a lot."

Alex nodded and walked over to me. "Sage, I want to show you something. Willow, can I borrow Sage?" he asked.

Willow nodded in agreement.

I shrugged and got up and waved goodbye to Willow. Alex led the way. I swore I would never see every tunnel. Just when I thought I had seen it all, there was somewhere or something new to see.

"Sage, you're supposed to be resting, but I heard you were training," Alex said.

"I couldn't rest. I couldn't sit still, then Willow found me."

Alex stopped in front of a beautiful door.

On it was the symbol of an open book. He opened the door and waited for me to go in. I walked in, stunned.

The Library

A Hidden Message Long Forgotten

The room was a library. A massive library. Shelves upon shelves were lined with books. Signs hung from the ceiling with detailed descriptions of different book genres. I ran my hand along the wall and picked a book on fairy potions. The cover had intricate designs and coloring. I walked further down the shelf and looked at a book about how the Fairy Tree was made.

I slipped it back in its place and picked out another book. I kept going, and soon days flew by. Before I knew it, Phenyx was healed, and I had read a whole shelf of books. Alex said I was in there for just about a week. I thought I had read almost every book in the library.

One day, I came across a book that had been slipped deep into the shelf. Almost invisible between the others. If I didn't know better, I would have thought someone had been trying to hide it from others. The cover said, "History on The Five Fairy Tribes." It had a delicate cover that appeared old, almost ancient. I ran my hand across the front and could feel the details of the worn designs, like bumps on tree bark. With every touch, I feared the book might crumble. I had never heard about the five fairy tribes, so I opened the book carefully, afraid I might destroy its contents. As it opened, dust and a small piece of paper fell to the ground. The piece of paper was the top left corner of a page, burned around the edges. Did someone try to destroy this book? This page?

I bent down and picked it up. I began to read:

You've opened a door you cannot undo. For the path you now face, your heart must be true. Dark and deep waters in which you may drown, by the hands of a princess who wears a golden crown. There awaits a deep secret where magic aligns. A friendship in the day will show you the signs.

I took the book over to Alex. "What's this all about?" I asked.

Alex gently took the paper from my hand. All he could say was, "Oh no…"

Aurora, Jones, Alex, and I were gathered in the library. The door was locked behind us. Aurora looked at the book in disbelief, taking the paper from Alex.

"Sage, you have discovered an ancient prophecy," Aurora said. "I don't know who or what put this there, but it turns out you are part of this prophecy." She paused. "There are five fairy tribes. First, there is the Sky Tribe. Their wings are built to blend in with the sky. They use spears as a weapon, and they can breathe at high altitudes. Next is the Woodland Hunter tribe. They blend perfectly into their forest environment. They are amazing hunters. Next is the Barbaric tribe. They ride horses on the empty, grassy plains. They use axes as their weapon. Then you have the Hidden tribe. We are that tribe, Sage. We live hidden beneath human feet, and we use many different weapons."

I counted the tribes on my fingers. I only counted four. "What about the fifth tribe?"

Aurora took a deep breath, "The fifth tribe is the Corrupt Tribe of magic fairies. Their leader, Lady Gwendolyn... is my sister. She is a sorceress. A very powerful one. She gets her power from the world's chaos, death, and destruction. Sage, you must go on a quest to join with three other fairies, one from each tribe. You must join together with them to defeat my sister. But know this, she is the one destroying the earth, making it what it is now. If you can find all of the pieces of the prophecy and put them together, you can unlock immense power to end my sister. The prophecy tells you what tribe to go to first. Can you guess?"

I re-read the prophecy.

You've opened a door you cannot undo. For the path you now face, your heart must be true. Dark and deep waters in which you may drown, by the hands of a princess who wears a golden crown." There are no tribes with water, though," I said.

"The Sky Tribe. They create the weather. They use water as the key ingredient. Go there first," Aurora said. "Now, go pack your bags. You must leave soon.

Gwendolyn will sense the prophecy being found. She will destroy the other pieces if she knows you have found a part of it. That will prevent you from ending her destruction. You need all the pieces. Go, go now!"

I sprinted out of the library, forgetting that there was a door. I ran into it headfirst. I staggered backward, rubbing my head where there would soon be a big bruise. I hastily unlocked the door and ran out. I jogged up the stairs as fast as possible, tripping a few times. Once I got up the stairs, I ran to my room. I opened the door, not caring to shut it. I grabbed my bag and tossed some stuff in. I packed my arrow-making kit, my dagger sharpening rock, spare clothes, and my small but very helpful first aid kit. I was walking out the door when I realized I had forgotten a few more things.

I ran to my bed. Reaching under, I pulled out my sleeping bag and a small pillow. I stuffed them in my bag and ran out the door. I dashed to get to the main tunnel.

Rushing over to the potion shelf, I grabbed all the potions on it. I stuffed them in my bag and moved on. I went over to the food room and packed as much as I could carry. I snatched a water canteen, a pot, and a ladle for cooking. I stuffed those in my bag, as well. On the way out, I grabbed some flint. I was forced to walk, not run, back down to the library because my bag was so heavy. I met Aurora, Jones, and Alex there. I walked in, pulling my bag behind me.

Aurora came up to me and pointed her staff at my bag. A second later, it felt as light as a feather. "Inside goes on forever, so now you can put almost anything in without all the weight."

I nodded, giving her my thanks. I walked over to Alex, giving him a big hug. Then, to Jones and hugged her, too. I went back to Aurora, who shook my hand.

"Bye, guys," I said while waving. "I'll see you soon." *I hope.* Why? Why me? I thought. Just when I was settling into fairy life, there had to be something to disrupt it. There just had to be a prophecy with me involved.

I went to find Phenyx and Willow. Phenyx was heating a bath with her powers. I snuck into her room and knocked on the bathroom door. A few moments later, she came out and hugged me.

"There's something I need to tell you," I said, moisture beginning to form in my eyes as I looked at her.

Phenyx sat down across from me as I told her everything. The prophesy, the book... the truth. It was difficult, but necessary.

"I want you to have something," Phenyx said. "I don't know if it will help you, but I'd like to think that it will. Go dig under my bed, and you'll find a dagger in a sheath."

I did as she said and rummaged around under her bed until I felt it. I brought it out and held it. Its sheath was made of cold leather, it felt as frigid as snow. The leather was as smooth as a polished stone. I pulled the dagger out of its sheath. It glowed red, orange, and yellow. The dagger radiated heat and had ancient fairy runes on it. I reached to touch it, but Phenyx grabbed my hand and yanked it back.

"That dagger was made by the Fire Ancient. He came with many others long before the fairies were split into tribes. Other Ancients are still out there. At least some people think they are. He made this dagger out of the first fire. It's hot as the sun itself. This dagger can cut through anything. I want you to have it. Considering that I have fire powers, I don't need this anymore." She closed my fingers around the sheath. "But you can't touch the blade, or it will burn you badly. This sheath is made from the Ice Ancient, it's meant to keep the dagger from burning you. That's why it's cold. Please keep it. You don't have to give it back. Now, go save the world." A tear fell down her cheek.

Phenyx gave me one last hug and pushed me out the door. I waved one last goodbye and went to find Willow. I ran around the burrow, looking for her, but she was nowhere to be found. There was one last place to look. I ran back down the tunnel I had come from and ran to Willow's room, getting lost a few times. Finally, I found it. Her door was marked with a willow tree and made of oak wood. I opened the door and headed for her blank wall. I pushed on it, revealing the hidden entrance, and walked in.

I found Willow sitting at her table next to the masterpiece she had made. She looked up and saw me. She grabbed the dry masterpiece and held it out. It was as smooth as marble, and it was us! We were holding each other and smiling together. I looked at it and tried not to cry.

Before I could, Willow ran up and gave me a big hug. "Alex told me everything. Go save the world. I know you can," she whispered.

I nodded and left the room, smiling as a tear rolled down my cheek. I went to the burrow's entrance and saw Alex waiting for me. Hands outstretched, he handed me the book and the prophecy. I took the book carefully out of his hands and slid it into my bag. I gently picked up the prophecy and put it into a small pocket. I went to Alex and gave him one last hug before walking out of the burrow. Once outside, I pulled the prophecy out of my satchel.

I read it aloud, "You've opened a door you cannot undo. For the path you now face, your heart must be true. Dark and deep waters in which you may drown, by the hands of a princess who wears a golden crown. There awaits a deep secret where magic aligns. A friendship in the day will show you the signs."

A blue ball of light flew out of the prophecy as I finished reading. It flew off to the south. With one last look at the burrow, I took a breath. What if my heart isn't true? I sure don't want to drown. What if Aurora is wrong? Maybe the book selected the wrong fairy to find it. After all, I'm hardly a fairy, I'm certainly not a hero ready to save the world. The blue ball of light was fading into the distance, almost too hard to see now. No time to waste.

Pushing off the ground, I flew south.

S. Hoffman

Epilogue

Long ago, before the fairies were split into tribes, there were The Ancients. When the world was first created, the Ancients were born. The stars blessed each Ancient with the power to control a particular element. And so, The Ancients gave life to the world. They made flora and fauna first, but soon they grew lonely. They then created The Fairy Tree. The tree was covered in pink leaves, and its blossoms were a hot pink hue. Every year, the tree would give The Ancients a bundle of baby fairies.

For years, The Ancients raised these fairies and blessed them with magic gifts. Then, one day, the Ancient, who controlled all despair, anger, hate, sorrow, and every bad feeling in the world, divided the fairies. She divided the Ancients, too. She split the fairies into five tribes. The Hidden Tribe, the Sky Tribe, the Woodland Hunter Tribe, the Barbarian Tribe, and the Corrupt Tribe.

The Ancients were scattered across the world… never to be seen again, and the fairies were divided across the globe. For generations, the Tribes have tried to forget each other. But soon, that may change…

About the Author

Scarlett Hoffman is a 12-year-old first-time novelist. She came into writing during the COVID-19 pandemic and soon found herself immersed in the storytelling of this epic adventure that will share the fates of the fairy tribes. Scarlett is an avid reader and loves Sci-Fi and Dystopian novels. She especially loves reading while holding her pet cat, Shadow. She is looking forward to sharing the rest of the fairy adventures in the remaining books of this series.

Please visit Scarlett at:

https://www.instagram.com/scarlett_hoffman_books/

https://www.facebook.com/profile.php?id=100083044375046

https://www.anatolianpressllc.com/scarletthoffman

https://www.anatolianpressllc.com/

The Lost Fairy Chronicles Book II: The Adventures of Wren D'laire

Have you ever felt different from everyone else? Were you born with a unique… gift? Maybe it doesn't feel like a gift, but more of a curse. A heavy burden only you can carry. My name is Wren D'laire. Technically, Princess Wren D'laire, daughter of Queen Elora D'laire, and rightful heir to the throne of my kingdom. The kingdom of Azalia. I was born with a gift that was treasured by everyone in my kingdom. My gift is… Wait! Mother would never let me tell you. So, I won't. But I will tell you a little of my story.

When I was born, the nurses told my mother that I wasn't going to live. Mother held me in her arms, tears rolling down her cheeks and onto my chest. Suddenly, there was a flash of sky-blue light, and the tears that soaked my body began to float in the air and glow with the light of a thousand stars. All the teardrops began to move toward me. The water went into the skin on the palm of my dying hand, and I suddenly took a deep, shuddering breath. Mother knew that The Ancients had blessed her with a gift that day. They saved an innocent life, and in return, I would eventually save even more. But for a price. Since the Ancients saved my life and blessed me with a magic gift, they took my wings in return. I lost the one thing that made a fairy, a fairy…only to get a magic blessing. I guess now I am just a small human – a small human princess with a gift.

Then she came. She came to conquer our kingdom. To force us under her reign. My kingdom is controlled by a horrible villain named Gwendolyn. She wants to bring death and destruction to this world to get revenge. Before Gwendolyn let evil consume her, she was my mother's friend. Now, Gwendolyn (or Gwen, as my mother used to call her) wants death. Death to everyone who harmed her. She will stop at nothing to get what she wants, even if it means destroying the world in the process.

Coming Summer of 2023

Made in the USA
Monee, IL
30 November 2022